# MURDER IN BEACON HILL

Utterly Addictive 1930s Cozy Mystery

Massachusetts Cozy Mystery
Book 5

ANDREA KRESS

© ANDREA KRESS 2024

Created with Vellum

## Chapter 1

Amanda Burnside descended the staircase in her family's Beacon Hill home with a spring in her step as she looked forward to the day. Although the weather was the normal cold, gray January, she had that spark of excitement that comes from starting a new job. It wasn't actually new—she had been sorting through the jumble of paperwork that the investigator at her father's law firm had left behind the previous month. But with the start of a new year, the partners had seen fit to find the funds in the budget to hire her on a part-time basis.

*For now*, she said to herself.

The smell of coffee wafted out of the breakfast room, and she picked up the scent of what might have been pancakes or waffles, something at which Cook excelled.

"Morning, Mother," she said, stooping to peck her mother on the cheek. She went behind her father's chair and kissed him on the cheek while looking over his shoulder at the newspaper.

"Financial pages. Nothing good to see here," he muttered.

"I heard on the radio that WPA has created jobs for people. That's a good thing, isn't it?"

"Yes, and luckily no one in this family has got to go begging for work."

Mrs. Burnside pursed her lips as Amanda sat down and poured herself a cup of coffee.

"And that's why I wonder why you think you have to go out and get a job," she said to her daughter.

"Mother, we've been through this. I'm helping the firm out and earning my own pin money to boot."

"And I'll make sure that she's not exposed to anything untoward," Mr. Burnside said from behind the paper, not able to see Amanda's exasperated expression.

"Ooh—what am I missing?" her sister Louisa asked as she came into the room. "Morning, all."

"It's not as if I'll be tracking down murderers," Amanda said. Her comment was met by the other three family members staring at her. "Well, the recent business in Hyannis was entirely a fluke." She muffled the last words with a sip of coffee.

"Just your average miscreants, I suppose. Daddy, I've never thought of this before, but what is a creant?" Louisa asked. "And we say people are ruthless, but what does it mean to be ruth?"

"I seem to recall that it means 'friend' in Hebrew," he replied. He folded the newspaper and put it beside his plate. "So, you can use it in a crossword sometime."

"Good to know," replied Louisa, who never did crossword puzzles. She patted her hair into place.

They ate in silence for a few minutes before Mrs. Burnside asked Louisa, "What exciting things are happening at Monsieur Josef's this week?"

"Women are coming in to place orders for the Valentine Ball. You ought to make an appointment soon or we'll be booked up."

"I thought I'd wear my dress from last year."

Louisa's eyes opened wide, and she put her fork down onto her plate dramatically. "That's not possible. Every deb and her mother know that I design for the chicest women's salon in Boston. You can't show up at the ball in what you wore last year. Everyone will think our family can't afford a new gown."

"With the price of those tickets, I'm surprised anyone can afford it," her father said.

"It's for Mercy Hospital, remember?"

"Who can forget Mercy Hospital?" Amanda said with a smirk. She had volunteered and then worked there before the Director left to take another job. The new administration didn't think that Amanda's projects of extending the free children's clinics to other neighborhoods was worth the expense and had eliminated her job. Although she had hard feelings about it, she was pleased that her father had taken umbrage at the untimely termination and asked her to help sort out the chaos of the firm's investigator who had abruptly left. *That's what family is for,* she thought.

Mr. Burnside got up. "Ready to go in about twenty minutes?" he asked Amanda.

"Yes, Mr. Burnside."

Her mother looked puzzled.

"I can't very well call him Daddy at work."

"And I can't possibly be ready so soon," Louisa said.

"Very well. Amanda, why don't you ferry your sister to the salon so I can get going."

"Yes, Mr. Burnside. I'm just practicing, Mother," she said in response to her mother's continued surprised look. "As you know, it's an old firm, very conservative and staid." Then she added, "Nothing untoward ever happens there, I'm sure."

It wasn't too long before Amanda was to find out that wasn't entirely true.

## Chapter 2

It was more than an hour before Louisa was fully dressed, made up and felt appropriately accessorized for her day.

"Whew," Amanda said, having observed the entire process finally at its conclusion.

"The women who come into Monsieur Josef's have high standards. And more importantly, they have lots of money to spend." She readjusted a blonde curl above her temple and pinned it in place. "I can't very well appear in a housedress."

Amanda laughed. "I'm working for one of the most prestigious law firms in Boston and I would hardly call my exquisitely tailored, wool crepe suit a housedress." She stood to position herself behind her sister to get a glimpse of her outfit in the mirror. "I suppose I could do a bit more with my coiffure, though," she added, observing her bobbed hair.

"Not now. It's getting late."

"I thought that beauty takes time," Amanda said with a smile.

"The fashion day doesn't start as early as the drudgery of a law firm. But I do have to observe the opening hour," Louisa said. "After all, I am sometimes required to work late on a last-minute task."

"I thought those late evenings were spent at the Oasis," Amanda said, referring to Louisa's boyfriend's nightclub. "I can't imagine you sitting in a chair in some garret sewing buttons on evening dresses by the light of a candle."

Louisa flicked her sister on the arm. "I do the designs, my dear. Others sew on the buttons."

They descended to the garage by the backstairs, exited into alley and joined the other cars on the street making their way to the business district.

Sometime later, as she pulled to the curb in front of the salon, Amanda said, "If you need a ride home, call me."

"Wait, first come in. I want you to see something very special I'm working on."

She was late already but thankfully part-time. Amanda reasoned a few more minutes wouldn't hurt and followed her sister through the opulent double doors into the lobby that had the hint of expensive perfume. They took the elevator up to the top floor.

"The garret," Louisa muttered with a sidelong glance at her sister.

The large space had north-facing windows that gave the room the perfect artist's light for the women who were seated around several worktables. As Amanda and Louisa stepped out of the elevator, they could hear rapid footsteps on the nearby staircase.

"I'm sorry I'm late," an out-of-breath young girl said as she lifted her head. "Oh," she added, thinking she might be encountering her supervisor.

"Just us chickens," Louisa said.

"Good morning, mademoiselle," she responded.

"Amanda is my sister. This is Mari. She and her mother are experts with a needle."

"Marigold," the young woman said, holding out a slender hand to greet Amanda. "Better get going."

An older woman seated at the table looked up and gave the young girl a stern glance.

"Sorry, Mama," Mari said and swiftly hung her outerwear on the coatrack in the corner.

"This way," Louisa said to her sister, who was staring at Mari because she reminded her of someone. "My little space is in here."

What she had to show Amanda was a sketch of an evening gown in deep pink with burgundy accents on the skirt and shoulders.

"Very nice, but don't you think there should be more to the bodice?"

"Such as?"

"Material covering the rest of your bosom, for example. Perhaps some sleeves."

"It's just a sketch. Look how thin I've made the figure, with an impossibly tiny waist. It's how you're supposed to draw it," Louisa said, "not what it will really look like when it's finished."

"Any special occasion?"

"The Valentine Ball, of course."

Amanda raised her eyebrows.

"What do you really think?" Louisa asked.

"I was going to say it was a bit much, but I think it's a bit too little."

"Honestly, you're sounding so dowdy."

"Maybe you could make Mother a dress in that burgundy color."

She received a withering glance in return. "Perhaps I could make you a pink dress with a high neck and bows down the front. Then we could look like some singing trio."

"Maybe I'll just wear some old thing I've worn before."

Louisa gave her another glare.

"Time to leave, I think," Amanda said. "Although the idea of a matching pink dress for me would be kind of cute."

"Bye."

Amanda chuckled. She loved to tease her sister about her pretensions when it came to fashion. She walked past the workroom and glanced back at Mari, who smiled in return. What was it about her?

## Chapter 3

Amanda nodded to the receptionist in the lobby of her father's law firm as she went to Gilbert's office. Well, it was her office now, although it still bore the mark of the quirky former investigator who had left suddenly for Denver for health reasons. Or so he said. Perhaps a potted plant might change the atmosphere, she thought.

She hung her coat in the closet and peered further into the dark recess, noticing for the first time a brown briefcase covered with dust. Had Gilbert forgotten about it or decided not to take it with him? She dragged it out and blew the dust off the top and found the leather flap that closed it to be locked. If only she had a set of lock picks! Instead, she took a nail file from her handbag and jiggled it in the keyhole to no effect before remembering that she had seen some keys in the top drawer of the desk. Feeling foolish, found a small key and it was the one that opened the briefcase.

Amanda looked down on a strange assortment of items. Binoculars, useful for spying from afar unless Gilbert had been a birdwatcher. Several magnifying glasses although one should have been enough. A large ink pad that was slightly dried out but no rubber stamp. She took out a round, unlabeled jar that seemed to contain power—gunpowder? Not that she knew what gunpowder looked like. Fishing around, she pulled out a cloth bag with a paintbrush inside and then deduced that it must be fingerprint powder. She pressed her index finger on the desk that someone had recently polished, dusted some powder on it with the brush and blew away the residue.

"How exciting!" she said aloud, seeing her fingerprint show up. "And then what are you supposed to do—take a picture? And match it to hundreds of other photographs of people who had the ill luck to have been arrested by the police? And who in the world had the miserable job of doing the matching?"

The only other object in the briefcase was a metal horn that narrowed to a neck at one end. It almost looked like an old-fashioned ear trumpet and suddenly Amanda smiled to herself and put the larger end against the wall with the smaller end in her ear. She heard mumbling from the adjacent room but couldn't distinguish any words.

"How in the world was this of any use?" she asked aloud.

There was a knock and her father put his head around the door and stared.

"What on earth? My grandfather had one of those," he said.

"I think that Gilbert may have used it in an attempt to listen in on conversations."

"My recollection is that even with the ear trumpet, we still had to shout into it. Well, that's not why I'm here. I wanted to know if you have everything you need and suggest that you have a meeting with the attorneys whose cases you have been working on to update them on your progress."

"Of course," Amanda said although she thought it obvious that's what she was there to do.

He smiled and closed the door and suddenly something clicked in her brain. Marigold. How many people were named Marigold? She went to the low bureau behind the desk and pulled out the Hatton file detailing the comings and goings of Mr. Hatton, whom Mrs. Hatton intended to sue for divorce with representation from the firm. She flipped through the sheets of notes and pieces of paper that Gilbert had produced. There it was. Marigold Gisriel. The name of one of the women that Mr. Hatton had regularly visited. It couldn't possibly be the young woman she met at Monsieur Josef's salon. She was so young. And why would she have to have a job doing tailoring if she was being supported by a wealthy man?

Amanda opened a desk drawer to pull out a telephone directory. She searched for Gisriel and found an address on Commonwealth, but the person's first initial was not M but E. Could it be the same person? How many people had that unusual last name? Judging from the directory, none. Gilbert's notes were from some time ago, making Amanda think that he had already reported this information to Mr. Van Eaton, the attorney who had taken on the client, but her curiosity about the connection between a young seamstress and Mr. Hatton was too much and she had to find out. She was about to go to Van Eaton's office but thought perhaps a phone call to his secretary to make an appointment was more professional.

"Miss Burnside here," she began. "I was wondering if Mr. Van Eaton would be available for an update on the Hatton file today?"

"Just a moment, I'll check his calendar." There was a pause. "He has a half hour at eleven if that would suit."

"Yes, thank you."

After she hung up, Amanda shuffled through the sheets of reports that Gilbert had assembled showing the dates when Mr. Hatton had been to the Gisriel home. At least she had an address where she could identify whom he had been seeing rather than a series of hotel rooms with the other woman. How did the man ever find the time to meet his business obligations and to be at home with his wife and two adult children—one of whom was a fellow debutante in Amanda's year and the other her ne'er-do-well brother, from what she had heard from friends? Maybe that's why his wife was seeking a divorce in the first place.

Amanda felt she projected confidence as she walked the corridors of her father's firm, wearing her smart, wool crepe suit and carrying the sheaves of papers in a folder. She greeted the secretary, who smiled but was perplexed about who this tall, self-assured, young woman was and what her job was.

After letting Mr. Van Eaton know that Miss Burnside was there and making a few pleasantries about the weather, the secretary said, "Who do you work for exactly?" It was a reasonable question from her perspective in that all the women in the firm were secretaries or members of the typing pool and reported to men.

"I'm more of a consultant to the firm," Amanda offered. "I've taken over Mr. Gilbert's cases until he returns." Not that she imagined he was coming back any time soon.

"Oh. Are you a private investigator?" The secretary's eyes were wide at coming to that conclusion.

"Yes, you might say," Amanda replied as Mr. Van Eaton opened the door to his office and ushered her in.

He was a handsome, young man with perfectly combed, blond hair. He was obviously intelligent, or at least well educated, according to the diplomas on his wall. But Amanda thought he had a distracted demeanor when he sat down as if wondering why he was there and what he should be doing. She was curious about how the firm got its clients and until that moment, she had never thought to ask her father. It was an old, established firm, occupying a large office in Boston's business district, and she knew her father made a good salary as well as a portion of the firm's revenue as a partner. Did people who could afford a lawyer immediately think of them? Did they mostly represent families with old money wondering how to structure their trusts and wills? How did a recent law school graduate fit into this picture unless he belonged to one of those families or expected to bring in business from other former graduates from Brown, as one of the diplomas attested. She would have to ask her father how it all worked. For the moment, however, she had to turn her attention to Mrs. Hatton's potential divorce.

"I'm not sure if I need to tell you this," Amanda began, "but I know the Hatton family because Doris and I came out the same year. I mean, I'm not intimately involved in her family's affairs or anything, and we are certainly not related. I just thought you should know that it won't affect my work on the case."

"Yes, of course. Thank you for telling me." He fidgeted with a cufflink, twirling it around.

"And I do apologize for being unavailable for some time in December. There was an unfortunate business with the death of a friend's father, and I assisted the family in…." She trailed off as she saw that his attention was on a paper on his desk and not what she was saying.

"Anyway, I'm back and I wanted to go over some of the details of the Hatton situation." She had decided to call it that rather than a case, which sounded like some sort of police procedural.

His eyes returned to hers as he caught the name. "Ah, yes, Mrs. Hatton." He held out his hand to receive the typed sheets that she had prepared from Gilbert's notes. "Thank you. I do appreciate being able to see all the information in some coherent form. The previous investigator would brief me orally, which meant I needed to take notes. Not the most efficient system."

"No, I thought not. And this way, since I've made carbon copies, you can keep the original and I can continue to add to the list of places and names of people with whom Mrs. Hatton's husband is interacting." She waited while he looked over the list and pinched his lower lip with his thumb and forefinger. He slowly turned to the second page and muttered. After five more minutes, he flipped the pages back into place.

"Don't you think it odd that he appears to be visiting two women on a regular basis?"

Van Eaton's blush started at his neck and crept up his jaw and into his cheeks. Amanda was torn between apologizing for being so blunt or pretending not to notice his discomfort. She went with the second option.

He cleared his throat. "Yes, a very active man, as it seems. His wife suspected as much, which is why she came to us in the first place." He didn't meet Amanda's eyes but looked somewhere in the middle distance.

"Do you think it would be helpful to her case to continue to do surveillance of him? Or do you think there is enough evidence here to support your position?"

He didn't respond at first and then said, "Oh, sorry, I was just thinking through the implications."

Amanda wondered what he meant by that. More material would build a stronger case and the firm's billing to Mrs. Hatton would increase. But unless Mr. Hatton settled before it went to trial, it would mean airing the family's dirty laundry in a public setting, probably something neither of them would want. She didn't relish being a part of a public trial since she might be called to testify, something that hadn't occurred to her before. Perhaps that was what her mother was afraid of. As she watched Van Eaton deep in thought, she wondered if he had ever been in trial before. Glancing up at his diplomas, he had only graduated from law school the previous spring. Six months working for the firm may not have prepared him for what might be labeled 'Society's Divorce Scandal of the Year' in the newspapers.

"Let me give this some thought," he said and held the papers out to her. She countered by showing him that she had duplicates. "Oh, yes."

"How much of this information does Mrs. Hatton know?" Amanda asked.

"She suspected something of the sort, but I did not give her the details. To spare her feelings."

Amanda smiled. "That was kind of you. However, don't you think if she knew the whole story, she might be more assertive as to her rights as the wronged wife?"

"That she might come away with a better settlement?"

"That's right."

"Good thinking."

"Well, I'll leave you to it. If you want me to pursue further evidence of alleged infidelity, I would be happy to do so." Amanda waited for his response, which was not forthcoming, so she stood, thanked him for the time and left the office.

As she walked back to her office, she thought back to her father's suggestion that she might consider law school. Based on her interaction with Van Eaton, all she could think is that she could do a much better job of representing a client's interest than he could with his vague statements. But of course, no firm in Boston would hire a female attorney, and certainly not in a divorce proceeding. She was just going to stay in her lane for the time being, she thought, as she looked down at the diamond engagement ring on her finger.

AMANDA HAD AGREED to meet Brendan, her fiancé and a police detective, at their favorite restaurant, Catalano's, for a late lunch. He was already seated, looking toward the door, when she came in and his look of pleasure at seeing her almost took her breath away. He gave her a kiss on the cheek, took her coat and held out a chair for her at 'their' table.

"As always, it smells so wonderful in here, don't you think, Sergeant Halloran?" she asked as he took her hand.

"I wasn't aware. I was too busy looking at you. Who gave you that extravagant ring?" he asked playfully, his blue eyes shining through the dark lashes.

"Just some admirer. I forget his name. It came in the mail. Isn't it sweet?"

"You'd better not forget his name since his very large family and circle of friends had been pushing to present it for some time."

"What? He couldn't make up his mind on his own?" she teased.

"Oh, he made up his mind a long time ago. He just didn't know how she would react."

"Welcome, lovebirds," the owner said as he approached their table. "How nice to see you on this very cold day."

"We know that a bowl of the Italian wedding soup to start with will help take off the chill," Brendan said.

"Just a cup for me, thank you," Amanda said. "I need to leave room for the main course."

"Let me put the order in while you make up your minds. Would you like a glass of wine?"

They both responded no, thinking of how sleepy it might make them for the afternoon of work ahead.

"How is your first official day at work?" he asked her.

"Very interesting. I was rooting around in the closet and came across Mr. Gilbert's briefcase. Inside were all sorts of very odd stuff."

"Such as?"

"Binoculars."

"To be expected."

"Magnifying glasses."

"Was there a deerstalker hat in there, too?"

"Don't be ridiculous. I thought the ear trumpet was strange enough."

Brendan looked up at her. "What?"

The owner brought a tray with their soup and a breadbasket and scurried away, one eye on the door in anticipation of other diners.

"You know. Those things that people hard of hearing put up to their ears to hear better."

"Was he hard of hearing? That could be a significant disability in his line of work."

They each began to eat the steaming soup.

"No, I think he may have used it to try to listen in on conversations that were happening in an adjacent room," Amanda said.

"Like the old trick of putting a glass against the wall."

"Exactly."

"Except that never works."

"Neither does the ear trumpet so I found out. And there was an ink pad. Like the kind I've seen at the police station when they take your fingerprints."

"That makes no sense. First, someone would have to agree to do that, and then what? He didn't have access to the police fingerprint file. And trying to make a match is a tedious and imprecise exercise. Even the specialists sometimes admit that partials, smudges and distortions get in the way of clean match."

"And fingerprint dust. I got to try it out on my own index finger. You know, what your folks do when they visit a crime scene."

"Again, that would be of no use to him unless he had some contact on the inside who could get that information analyzed. Now I'm beginning to wonder what sort of work he was actually up to. Not just divorce cases and financial shenanigans." After a pause he said, "I think I might take a look into his background."

"As you know, he's not even in the state anymore. Moved to Denver for his health. So he said."

Mr. Catalano, who had been hovering near the entrance, noticed they had finished their soup and came forward to clear the table and ask about their entrees.

"I'll have the tagliatelle with salmon," Amanda said.

"The chicken piccata for me," Brendan said.

Mr. Russo nodded his head and smiled, as he always did, no matter what they ordered.

"What's new at work?" Amanda asked Brendan.

"Since we last talked two days ago, not much. The usual full cells from everyone's need to overdo things and misbehave over the weekend. And then the subsequent paperwork to process them back onto the street puts most of the force in a bad mood. Monday mood we call it."

"Do you think there is more rowdiness now that Prohibition is over?"

"Surprisingly, not particularly."

"I've often wondered how Rob Worley manages to keep things calm at the Oasis," Amanda said.

"There is a type of man, usually a working man, who likes to have a few drinks and get in a fight just for the fun of it on a weekend night. And he knows exactly what kind of places to go to for that sort of entertainment. It does not include potted palms, a band playing swanky numbers and an elegantly clad female singer. Nor burly, menacing-looking employees who can prevent an altercation starting."

Amanda laughed. "I guess you have a better eye for those kinds of things. I've never noticed anyone who looks intimidating, except maybe Aldo. Louisa said he's actually a sweet man with a wife and several children."

"I think the thing that surprises me is that everyone seems to think that what Rob does for a living is benign. His charming demeanor, good looks, impeccable wardrobe and, of course, Louisa Burnside as his inamorata sitting ringside can gloss over anything."

Amanda had been reaching for a piece of bread but stopped. "What do you know that you're not telling me?

And don't give me that innocent, altar boy look."

"What? I was never an altar boy. Nor innocent, either, if I admit it. I'm just saying that owning a nightclub is a difficult business and he must deal with any number of rough characters. I'm not talking about the customers."

Amanda scanned his face, looking for clues about what he had said, but he was absorbed in buttering his bread.

"During Prohibition, we all knew that he was serving alcohol. But who wasn't? Are you suggesting something else?"

"I am supposing that he must have dealt with bootleggers and possibly even mobsters. His place seemed suspiciously immune to raids."

"Except for that one time," Amanda reminded him.

"Remember that no one was arrested. It was just a warning of some kind. I don't mean to sound cynical—."

"Heavens, no!"

"But you can't be in that kind of business without having to have protection. And I don't mean burly bouncers standing at the entrance with arms crossed over their chests. I'm sure he pays someone for protection."

"Why are you telling me this now?"

"I'm concerned for your sister. Your parents may have reservations about Rob Worley on social class grounds, but perhaps they haven't considered that he likely associates with dangerous people."

The owner brought their plates to the table, presenting them with a flourish. "Is there anything else just now?"

"No, thank you," Brendan said. After Mr. Catalano had stepped away, he said to Amanda, "Let's not talk about Rob if that unsettles you."

"All it does is give me room for thought. In the meantime, could you recommend where I could purchase a set of lock picks?"

## Chapter 4

Mrs. Hatton was feeling very self-assured as she made her way into Monsieur Josef's salon wearing a black suit with a nipped-in waist and a fur coat against the icy winds. She had always been admired for her petite frame and tiny feet and she walked slowly toward the entrance as if on a runway as she gave a benign smile to the doorman. She was here to order a gown for the Valentine Ball next month and, aside from excitement about that, she was flushed from her latest encounter with young Mr. Van Eaton. Not only was he representing her in an impending divorce, but he also seemed to have taken a romantic interest in her. No, it wasn't some silly, middle-aged woman imagining things; he went above and beyond what a lawyer usually did and came to the house in Beacon Hill and had long conversations with her about her life, her dreams and her future. Something her husband could not be bothered with.

Every time her husband came into her thoughts, she shooed him away. Not only did he not pay any attention to her anymore, but she had come across a bill from a florist's they didn't usually use for an order of gardenias. And no such order had been delivered to their home. She called them, pretending to be her husband's secretary, and found out to whom they were sent—a name she didn't recognize. That was enough to send her into a determined quest to either get the attention of her husband back or get what she deserved from being his wife, mother of his children and the person who upheld their social position in society for these many years.

Getting his attention back had proved to be pointless as he was always preoccupied with business, his club and worrying about their son's lack of ambition. She had moved onto the other alternative quickly. While divorce was a serious step with financial and social implications, she made up her mind that she was willing to take it. She would keep the house, have alimony and, if whispers of his infidelity got about—which she would be sure to plant—she would be painted the long-suffering victim.

But timing is everything and she had not pulled the trigger yet. She was going to order a gown for the Valentine Ball and enjoy herself enormously at that event. She told Van Eaton that she would wait until after that important social event to officially sue for divorce. Having seen them as a couple at the upcoming event, society would be shocked, but certainly on her side, when they became aware of his sordid activities. She intended to continue to be the loving, admiring wife until that bomb dropped, and she was certain that sympathy would be on her side and result in a generous settlement. While being a divorcee had a tinge of glamor about it, in her case, there could be nothing to fault her behavior. And who knows? There might be an admirer who would step forward in the future. After all, she might be middle-aged, but she was elegant, well connected and soon to be independently wealthy.

Monsieur Josef came forth into the lobby to welcome her with open arms that then encircled her hands and gave them a kiss.

"Madame, you are looking radiant! There must be some wonderful thing in your life to give you such a glow."

She blushed a bit and said, "Life is wonderful. I have a loving husband and two accomplished children. The only thing lacking is a gown for the Valentine Ball. You know my daughter had her debut there, and how can we not support Mercy Hospital? It may be a cold and gray January, but let's look forward to a lovely spring."

With that, they proceeded into the showroom as if in a procession, and he sat her down in a chair and offered refreshment.

She giggled. "A bit early, don't you think?"

Monsieur Josef chuckled in return. He was thinking of coffee but snapped his fingers at his assistant to bring a glass of champagne.

"We have some designs to show you, of course, but I've recently hired a designer and I would be happy to have her work with you on something unique. Something utterly yours."

At this point, Louisa came into the room with a sketchpad and introduced herself.

"Of course, I know you. Your sister, Amanda, came out with Doris."

"Yes," Louisa said. "The family has long been supporters of Mercy Hospital. Now that I've seen you in person again, I think I may have to alter some of my sketches. I had no idea you were so petite and certainly was not aware of your periwinkle blue eyes. We must have the gown in that color to accentuate them and the golden hue of your hair."

Louisa produced some colored pencils and drew them across the bottom of the page where she had a sketch of a gown with a solid bodice and skirt and glittering sheer sleeves.

Mrs. Hatton gasped. "That's beautiful. It would be perfect. I know many women think they should wear red for the Valentine Ball, but this would turn things on their head. To respect Monsieur Josef, however, I think I should see what he had in mind with the models first."

"Absolutely," Louisa said, knowing that what she had presented was far more suitable than what the models would be wearing.

The assistant reappeared with a coupe glass of champagne that she carefully handed over to Mrs. Hatton along with a cloth napkin. She almost purred in contentment.

Although the designs that the models paraded in front of her were perfectly acceptable for the occasion, either the cut or the color was not suitable. She thought the green dress would make her pale complexion and blonde hair look sallow. And the embellished red dress would make her look like a Christmas ornament well past its season. She liked the design of the white dress and thought it would flatter her figure, but all the debs wore white, and it would be ludicrous for someone of her age to appear to be competing with the young women. She thought the dress

Louisa had shown her would be perfect but didn't want to give the girl a swelled head just yet.

"May I see the sketch again?" she asked and took her time examining every feature. "The fabric of the bodice and skirt?"

"I thought that satin would give a subtle shimmer."

"Hmm. And the sleeves?"

"Tulle or net."

Mrs. Hatton frowned a bit. "Let me think about it. May I see the green dress again?"

The model came back out and down the two steps to stand next to the older woman, allowing her to touch the fabric before tilting her head to one side as if debating with herself.

"Oh, this is so difficult." She sipped the champagne and gave Monsieur Josef a baffled look. "What do you think?"

"I think the choice is obvious. These other dresses come from reputable ateliers in Paris and London. But here you'll have a bespoke gown."

Mrs. Hatton dithered. "I do have some lovely diamond jewelry that would set it off nicely."

"Why don't we take your measurements and get an estimate of the yardage needed." He gestured to a door off the showroom that housed two dressing rooms, each with tufted chairs in the event a client brought someone with them for a fitting.

As she walked through the doorway, Monsieur Josef's eyes narrowed at Louisa. "Have you estimated the cost?"

"Of course," she answered.

Mrs. Hatton made her way into the first dressing room and was met by one of the assistants.

"Hello. I'm Mari," she said, closing the door and removing a measuring tape from around her neck while placing a notebook and pencil on a small round table. "There is no need to undress; I can do this over what you're wearing. But if you could remove the jacket. Thank you."

She took the jacket and placed it carefully on a hanger on a hook. "If you could tell me how tall you are, please." She jotted the number down on the pad. "And do you usually wear this height of heel?" She noted that as well, then got busy measuring bust, waist, hips, shoulder breadth, neck to waist, arm length before taking a yard stick and dropping it from Mrs. Hatton's waist to just above the ankle.

"There, all done." Mari picked up the suit jacket, noting the label and held it out for the woman to insert her arms. She could feel the woman's eyes on her and put on a smile, opened the door and gestured to the showroom. When she was by herself, she looked in the mirror to see if her cheeks were red or any emotion could be detected from her outer appearance. She wasn't about to let the woman know who she was, no matter what.

## Chapter 5

Brendan considered telling Amanda that he had to be back at the station so he wouldn't have to accompany her to the pawn shop, but he knew that she would go on her own and he couldn't let that happen.

"I appreciate that you want to protect me, but won't the owner be suspicious if he sees you? I mean, that kind of person must know every police officer in the city." She clung onto his arm as they rounded a corner into the full force of the wind.

"Not every police officer. Although whenever stolen goods are an issue, we do make the rounds. I do know Mr. Somers well, however."

Amanda looked over at him. "Has he received stolen goods in the past?"

"Unwittingly, he has said."

The notion of being an investigator was starting to become a bit more unsavory to her. But once begun on a path of action, she wasn't about to back out. She would see this excursion through.

Brendan took her to a shop on a side street in North End where three golden balls were suspended from the top door frame. They stood in the tiled entryway and heard the door unlock before making their way in. It was dark inside and barely warmer than the outside temperature. At the back of the store a short man, a stubby cigar jutting from the corner of his mouth, was in a wire cage.

"Look what the cat dragged in," he said in husky voice.

"Hey, Saul. Long time no see," Brendan said.

"Just as well."

They approached and felt the warmth of an electric heater inside his enclosure as he looked Amanda up and down.

"We're looking for something," Brendan said.

"Sure, sure."

Amanda took her gloves off to reach into her handbag and Mr. Somers had already observed the ring on her finger.

"It's over already, is it?" He put a loupe up to his eye and held out his hand through the opening in the cage as if to take her hand to examine the ring. He laughed loudly at his bad joke and her reaction.

Brendan looked at Amanda. She was going to have to do this on her own.

She cleared her throat. "I was wondering if you had any lock picks?"

He looked from her to Brendan and back again and cupped a hand behind one ear. "What?"

She repeated her request.

"That's what I thought you said. I can't imagine why you might think I had such items in my store."

Brendan gave an exasperated expression. "Okay, you're on the up-and-up. We know. But do you have any lock picks?" Not getting a response, he added, "She writes for those crime magazines and needs to see firsthand what they look like." Amanda shot him a look.

"Oh, in that case." He exited the cage and went over to a glass case at the far end of the store. "Surprisingly, I have a few."

"What a surprise," Brendan said.

Amanda looked at the sets of metal bars on rings rather than just one instrument or tool as she had expected. "This looks more complicated than I thought."

"Picking a lock is an art that requires practice. If you don't mind me asking, what do you intend to open?"

"I'm not sure yet. I thought I would familiarize myself with the process."

Saul looked at Brendan with eyebrows raised.

"Lemme ask you a question. If you was shipwrecked. I mean, if the crew of your ship went overboard, what would be the things you would most want to take with you into your little dingy? Water, an oar or a sextant?"

Amanda and Brendan looked at each other. What was he talking about?

"A sextant," she answered.

Saul let out a huge laugh. "That's what everyone says. Do you have any idea how to use a sextant?"

"No."

"I could sell you these lock picks, but do you have any idea how to use them?"

There was a pause. "I was hoping I could learn."

"How do you plan to do that? Wander around your fancy house—wherever that is—and fiddle around with the locked bedroom doors? What will the family think?" He burst into laughter and to her dismay, Brendan joined in.

Amanda could feel her face turning red and was relieved they were in such a gloomy spot in the store that perhaps neither of the men noticed.

"As I said before, you have to practice."

"Who could help me?"

"I'll sell you these at a deep discount. Come back in a day or two and either me or Eddie will show you the basics."

"Who's Eddie?" Amanda asked as she heard Brendan groan.

"He's a real pro and it takes a couple of years to be a pro, but I'm guessing you're not going to be breaking and entering any time soon. Not in that outfit, at least." He thought that so funny that he broke out in laughter again.

"Thanks for the advice," she replied.

Driving home in the cold, she wondered if there was some way she could learn the skills of an investigator—minus the lock picking. Not to mention safecracking. She felt her intuition was a great asset as was her relative fearlessness, and she couldn't discount Brendan's input and support. The only question was whether her father or his partners would consent to her continuing as their in-house investigator. Or she could seek someone else in the business as her mentor. But how to find that person?

Amanda's musings on her future had so absorbed her attention, that she almost forgot to pick up Louisa and made a quick left to turn back the several blocks to get her.

"Why so late?" her sister asked, climbing into the car.

"I hope you weren't waiting long."

"I was watching through the side windows. There was no way I'd stand outside on a night like this. Can't you turn the heat up any? Maybe we need a car rug."

Amanda laughed. "And here you go out to the Oasis in one of your flimsy evening gowns without a complaint."

"That's different. By the way, how would you like to drive me there tonight?"

Amanda laughed. "You can't be serious. Why can't Rob pick you up like a proper boyfriend?"

"Because he needs to be there—he's the reason people go to the club. He sets the tone, keeps people circulating and, more importantly, keeps the peace."

"I am loathe to suggest it, but on this one occasion, you may borrow my beloved vehicle."

"Really?"

"Once we've warmed up and had dinner, going out is the last thing I want to do. Just go easy on the martinis or whatever the drink du jour is."

Louisa leaned over and kissed her sister on the cheek.

"Don't get maudlin now," Amanda said with a smile.

LOUISA LEFT SOON after dinner was completed, accompanied by a scowl from her father who didn't approve of her going to a club, especially one that was owned by the man she had been seeing. Her floor-length, silvery crepe de chine dress had a bateau neckline and, with her long overcoat open at the front, disguised the plunging back as she came to the sitting room to say goodnight.

"That's lovely, dear. One or your designs?"

"Yes, Mother. Monsieur Josef has given me free rein to show off the finished work at the Oasis. Good for business, you know."

"I'm glad I didn't pay for that," Mr. Burnside said.

"Not only did you not pay for it, but I'm also bringing in a salary of my own. Don't you forget," she teased as he put the evening newspaper in front of his face with an audible grumble.

"Now that I'm a working girl, I'll be home early. Please don't worry." She was earnest in her intentions as having to get up for work each morning had given a regularity to her day that was missing previously.

She drove carefully and then saw the familiar neon image of a curved palm tree visible from the end of the block where cars were backed up, waiting to get into the parking lot. While Louisa knew that her parents did not approve of Rob and his business, he had been polite, respectful and attentive to her and them. And since Prohibition had ended, there was no taint of illegality in what he did, which she felt legitimized his standing.

When she approached the front canopy, one of the attendants dressed in what was supposed to make him look like a Middle Eastern potentate, complete with a feathered and bejeweled turban, white shirt and pants, addressed her by name, opened the door and took the car keys to park the car. Another similarly dressed man nodded to her and opened the doors to the warm and noisy interior of the club, decorated with actual palms and murals of the desert to set an exotic scene. The hat-check girl took her long overcoat, cooed over the dress and Louisa made her entrance.

Rob caught sight of her immediately and came to escort her to one of the front tables.

"How are you tonight?" he asked although he had seen her just the night before. "What a gorgeous dress."

"Thank you. One of my own designs."

"Perhaps Monsieur Josef would like to have a fashion show here one day."

"What a wonderful idea. Although he likes to show his wares to women buyers mostly and this, as you can see, is mostly a couples' audience."

"Perhaps with such an audience the man would purchase a gown for the accompanying girlfriend or wife?" Rob smiled, showing his perfect, white teeth in contrast to his face, slightly tan even in the winter.

There was a guffawing from a corner table of five men as they laughed at some joke, which prompted Louisa to ask, "Are those fraternity brothers? Are they even of legal drinking age?"

Rob laughed. "Since when are you concerned about whether we adhere to the rules?"

"Just being careful on your account," she said, settling herself in a seat at the small, round table.

"We refer to them as 'the lads.' Recent graduates of one prestigious college or another, in their first jobs—probably finance or law—and eager to spend their hard-earned money showing off to one another. Who could ask for better customers?"

"Why don't they bring dates?"

He shrugged.

"I think you should encourage them to do so. There are ever so many young women sitting at home bored when the lads could be enlivening their lives."

"Who might that be?" Caroline said, coming up to the table. They gave a distanced embrace while her husband, José, Rob's silent partner, bowed gracefully.

"Come sit with us. Have you just arrived?" Louisa asked.

"Yes," Caroline said with a drawl. "Long, tedious dinner at home." She sat in a chair opposite.

"Dinner was fine," José clarified. "It was the discussion with my brother-in-law, Fred, about his upcoming nuptials.

His inclination was for something simple, Spartan almost, and he was fighting the impulse of my dear mother-in-law and the wishes of the intended bride for a more elaborate affair."

"The age-old conflict. I say, do you know Valerie well? She was a few years behind me at school and seemed a bit of a mouse," Caroline said. "Fred hasn't brought her around much. Probably didn't want to scare her off."

"She was in Amanda's class and a fellow deb. Quiet, yes."

"Those are the ones to look out for, no?" José said.

"She used to be engaged to Emerson Something-or-other. She broke it off because he couldn't seem to settle on a career."

"Well, Fred is entrenched in his and he can be a stick, and then my mother is something else. I wish Valerie all the luck in the world," Caroline said, turning to see the maître d' approach to take their order.

"What's become of Sophia?" Louisa asked, noticing that the band was without a singer.

"Called in sick. I'm of the opinion that she's got her eyes on another gig," Rob said.

"I think people were getting a bit tired of her anyway," Louisa said, smiling at the possible exit of a woman who had set her sights so obviously on Rob.

Another outburst of laughter from the lads had the two couples turn their heads in that direction.

"We have got to find them some dates, José. First to tone down the noise and second to double the tab," Caroline said.

"We may double the tab briefly and suddenly the lads will not drink as much in front of their dates. Despite that, they will be scolded by the women for spending so much money. Soon they will be engaged and be at the women's houses planning the wedding. After the wedding, maybe one or two evenings out and then come the babies. No, leave it as it is."

José had the whole table laughing at his dire progression of events.

"Well, we're married and we're still here," Caroline noted.

"This is our business. We must always pay close attention to our investments. No matter what comes next for us, we'll always come to the Oasis."

"Which bigwigs are here tonight?" Louisa asked. "Present company not included, of course."

The maître d' brought three martinis to the table and asked if the party wanted anything more. Rob, who never drank on the job, was already nursing a seltzer, nodded that he had what he needed.

"The Mayor and the Police Chief are ensconced in one of the private rooms with a grim-faced gentleman. Who knows what that's about," Caroline said, taking a cigarette offered to her by her husband and waiting for him to produce a flame from a gold lighter. "What's new in the land of high couture?" she asked Louisa. "Is that one of your designs?"

"Of course. I couldn't be seen in public in something I picked up in Filene's."

They all chuckled at her remark.

"It's beautiful. I hope Monsieur Josef appreciates your artistry," Caroline said.

"I believe he does. Although just now the salon is swamped with requests for gowns for the Valentine Ball. Then, after cotillion season, it's the lead-up to the spring and summer weddings. He's busy all year round. I'm not complaining."

The band had stopped playing and, in the relative quiet of people talking, glasses clinking and silverware clattering on plates, the raucous laughter of the lads was even more pronounced.

"Do you think you should say something?" Louisa asked tentatively, not wanting to seem to interfere with Rob's business.

"I may not need to," he responded, glancing in their direction.

The door to the private room at the back had opened and the Mayor and Police Chief exited, neither holding a drink although they surely had been served; it was a matter of how things looked. They nodded to the customers in a generic way as if everyone should know who they were and proceeded slowly toward the table where Rob was seated. He stood up and gave a short bow, then shook the hands of both men who had stopped to chat.

The grim-faced man had followed them out of the room a few paces behind, looking entirely out of place in the youthful, celebratory crowd before his eyes lit upon the group of noisy young men. He stopped, stared and then approached the table, which instantly fell silent. Some words were addressed to the handsome, blond man who could barely meet the older man's eyes, but whatever was said made the table go quiet.

"There go four good customers," José muttered as he saw the young men leave their half-finished drinks and slink toward the front, followed by the older man, who seemed to want to make sure that they did leave.

"Who is that?" Caroline said aloud.

"One of my father's law partners," Louisa said.

## Chapter 6

The next day was Amanda's lunch with the X-D's as they called themselves, the debutantes who had come out together and had pledged to stay in touch, courtesy of Valerie's father's membership at a club that agreed to serve them in a private dining room. Mustn't have young women parading around just anywhere in a men's club, after all.

Amanda was one of the few who had any sort of job, some of them were still single and hoping to tie the knot in the near future, while a few of them were married and not living in Boston. The topics of conversation were usually about who wasn't in attendance, but discussion was kept at a non-malicious level—for who knew what might be said about oneself if absent at a subsequent luncheon?

Only Marnie was present when Amanda arrived on the dot of twelve. She was smoking, a known appetite suppressant since she had a very part-time position at Monsieur Josef's salon. They greeted one another with a kiss on the cheek and Amanda detected Chanel No. 5 emanating from her friend.

"I've been meaning to ask you for such a long time—why does everyone call it 'Monsieur Josef's' when it should be Monsieur Dubois? That is his name, isn't it?" Amanda asked. "Unless he really is Bob Smith."

Marnie gave a tinkling laugh. "Who knows? It seems the couturier business—and you'll never guess, they sometimes refer to it as the rag trade in New York—allows for all kinds of dramatic flourishes. One calls the client 'Madame' or 'Mademoiselle.' Jeanne's real name is Jean, of course. It's a good show that's put on. And now Louisa's under his spell." She blew a stream of smoke toward the ceiling.

"From what I understand, she seems to have a skill for design. Who knew?"

"Just yesterday, Doris's mother came in and, despite the best attempts to show the frocks that were on the racks from the New York and Paris houses, she chose Louisa's."

"How nice. She didn't mention it. I'm a bit jealous since I have no flair for artistic endeavors."

A waiter came in and took their drink orders and disappeared.

"Hello, hello," Valerie said coming through the doors of the room, her cheeks rosy from the cold. Each young woman received a peck on the cheek as Valerie removed her fur. "This weather!"

"Isn't it ridiculous that we say the same thing every January about the cold, and then every July we complain about the heat and humidity?"

Cecile walked in on the tail of the remark. "Hot and humid? Where? Take me there!"

They laughed at their friend, who always had a bon mot.

"What's new with you?" Marnie asked.

"Some news, but you'll have to wait until everyone is here so I can wallow in the congratulations."

The other women let out oohs and aahs in anticipation of what they were to hear. Cecile lit up a cigarette and smirked at them.

The others came in shortly thereafter, apologizing for being late, complaining about traffic, taxis and the cold. Doris and Ava, who hadn't been able to attend the December luncheon, demanded to know what they had missed.

"Nothing. Just our dull little lives. Except for Patricia, who had been on a cruise."

"Yes," Patricia said. "And my tan is fading already."

"As is your lightened hair!" Cecile added.

They all laughed, the object of the barb included.

"What news, everyone? Are we all here?" Valerie asked knowing that there was always an extra place set for someone who forgot to RSVP although there was usually one who said she would attend and didn't. "Amanda?" she asked with a smile, in part because she was herself now engaged to marry Fred Browne, Amanda's ex-boyfriend. She waited for Amanda's news to be announced.

"Yes, engaged." There was a round of clapping and appreciative noises as Amanda showed off her engagement ring, taking in the lukewarm looks for the less-than-required size that most had anticipated.

"When is the wedding?"

Amanda scoffed. "Hold on, everyone. We've only just got this far."

Ava sniggered.

"That's not what I meant," Amanda said, blushing.

That got everyone laughing, Amanda included.

"How about you, Valerie?" she asked. The laughter increased. "I meant—the progress on the wedding plans."

"Good save!" someone said.

Valerie flattened her left hand on the table, gazing at her sizable engagement ring, and pursed her lips. "With so many of you as my friends—and Fred having so many as well, we decided to keep things simple and just have Caroline as matron of honor and José as best man."

That stopped the laughing as everyone realized why that was the case. Valerie hadn't any sisters to serve as maid of honor and so chose her future sister-in-law, but Fred's brother was not available as he sat in a prison cell in Vermont. But that was another story. So, the brother-in-law would serve instead.

Jumping into the silence, Cecile said, "We'll be sitting in the front pews on the bride's side, cheering you on."

"Hear! Hear!" was the rousing addition from everyone, lifting their water glasses.

Two waiters rolled a trolley in with the sort of luncheon food the club thought young women would most enjoy: chicken salad, hearts of lettuce with French dressing, Parker House rolls and fruit cup. The women were talking quietly while being served, awaiting the departure of the waiters in order to hear further news from each member of the group.

When the trolley was rolled out and the doors closed, Betsy jumped in with her burning question. "All right, Cecile. You've held us in your thrall long enough. What's your news?"

Cecile had just taken a bite of buttered roll so held up a finger to ask for a pause. Everyone knew she was toying with them. After she swallowed, she said, "I'm sorry, what was your question?"

She was roundly booed by her friends.

"If we weren't eating in this club, I might have thrown my roll at you!" Doris said.

Cecile cleared her throat. "There is serious interest from a certain person who goes to Brown," she said.

"Your brother's roommate?" Patricia asked.

"As a matter of fact, you're correct."

"Could we have some clarification on 'interest?'"

"I'm afraid that's all I can say." Cecile resumed eating.

"Just look at that Cheshire cat grin!" Doris said. "Be careful, there are all those Pembroke girls around the Brunonians. Maybe you should rethink going to college."

"A four-year sentence?" Cecile asked. "No thanks."

"It could be less if you were to get your MRS."

Ava, who had been fairly quiet up until then, asked Amanda, "What's this I hear about a new job?"

"What do you hear?"

"My uncle is in your father's firm, so the cat is out of the bag."

All eyes were on Amanda. "I was working at Mercy Hospital and then the Director decided to leave and the Board in their infinite kindness in trying to cut corners cut out my job."

"No!" was the response from a few who hadn't heard about it until then.

"And the clinic expansion, too," Valerie said.

"My father's firm had just lost their investigator and I agreed to help out for a while. That started last month, and now I officially have a job there."

Marnie gasped. "Are you a private eye, as they call it? Like Sherlock Holmes?"

"Or Charlie Chan?" someone else asked.

"It's not that glamorous or dangerous. It's mostly reviewing paperwork," she said.

"Oh, I was hoping for some juicy gossip," Marnie said.

"If I had any, I wouldn't be able to share it."

This was met with groans of disappointment.

"Speaking of detection," Betsy began. "Isn't your brother's roommate Kit Hatton?"

"Aha!" Patricia said.

"I can't seem to remember," Cecile said slyly.

"You can be my Doctor Watson, Betsy," Amanda said.

"I'd like to help, but they don't portray him as very bright although he must be if he was a doctor. Or Number One Son. But he didn't seem to get what was going on much, either. Have you all seen the latest Charlie Chan movie?"

They broke into smaller groups talking about the latest movies and the activities of those who hadn't been able to attend the luncheon. Amanda responded with the appropriate level of attention, but she was wondering about the impending dissolution of the Hatton marriage and how that might affect Kit. And by extension, Cecile's hopes of a more permanent situation. All that was about to change.

## Chapter 7

The long lunch and vacuous conversations had given Amanda a headache, and she bowed out of work for the remainder of the afternoon. The idea that passing up on college had been a mistake had been nagging in the back of her mind for some time and meeting with her former debs had driven that home even more. She decided it might be something to explore by taking a class or two since she didn't have a full-time job. Tuition would be affordable, and she could still live at home; she would feel a little silly living in a dorm with a bunch of eighteen-year-olds. But what would she study? And as her father would ask, what was her goal? Not to be a teacher. She didn't have the patience for that. But what other occupations did women take on that might be of interest? Her cousin Aggie had been wise to do nursing—it suited her, and she was doing well. Should she even be considering college or a career when she was engaged? Why was life so complicated?

The house was quiet when she came in, and she managed to get up to her room without notice. She took her shoes and suit jacket off and slipped her feet under the satin bedspread, commanding her brain not to think of anything.

Tapping awakened her sometime later and she turned to see Louisa put her head around the door in the darkened room.

"I hope I haven't slept through dinner," Amanda said. Looking at the alarm clock beside her bed she saw it was only five o'clock.

"Tough day?" Louisa asked.

"X-deb lunch."

"Ugh. I don't see why you bother to keep up with those catty girls."

Amanda laughed and turned on the bedside light. "Have a seat," she said, patting the bed as she moved into an upright position. "After today's conversations about who was seeing whom, who was going where and having them look at my ring with disdain, I'm beginning to wonder. When someone complimented it as 'sweet,' she made it sound like a toy out of a gumball machine."

Louisa laughed. "Was Valerie flashing hers around?"

"Of course. Fred was always so careful with money—or at least complaining about the lack of it and having to live with his mother and sister. And then he springs for this rock. Rather vulgar, actually."

"Meow!" Louisa said.

Amanda had to laugh at herself. "Touché. It just irritates me that she acts as if she should feel sorry for me that she snatched Fred away, when everyone knows that we dated but it was all over between us before they became an item. From now on, I can be kindly condescending because she is stuck with him."

"And with his mother and the in-laws. Can you imagine living like that all crammed into the same house?" Louisa asked.

"From my experience working in some of the neighborhoods, there are quite a lot of people living like that. We're in the minority."

"Out of necessity, I can understand. But by choice? No privacy, and that weird mother."

Amanda swung her legs off the bed and put on her shoes and reached for her suit jacket. "That's not my concern anymore." She went to the vanity and looked at herself in the three-part mirror. "I've certainly mashed my hair." She sat down in front of the dainty, kidney-shaped, fabric-edged structure, picked up a hairbrush and attempted to get her bob in shape. Some powder and lipstick completed the repair needed after the nap.

"What smells so good?" she asked.

"Cook has rustled up a crown roast of pork. Perfect for a cold, nasty night."

Amanda went to one of the windows and looked out onto a distant streetlight and at what appeared to be sleet. She shivered. "Let's go down."

A fire had been lit in the sitting room and their mother was reading the morning newspaper, leaving the evening edition for her husband to peruse when he got home.

"There you both are! As quiet as mice—I didn't even know you were both home, although I could have checked to see if the car was here. I didn't even manage to get out today and, based on the weather report, I don't regret it at all. I remember when they had us wear woolen leggings that matched our coats in the winter. Somewhat itchy but much warmer than just hose and the shorter skirts that you all wear. How have you two fared?"

"Things are so busy at the salon, Mother. I really want to get some decisions from you about the Valentine Ball gown since women are already putting in orders."

Mrs. Burnside sighed. "I dread the entire process. I've gotten to be so plump."

This was a familiar complaint of hers and her daughters rallied to assure her that it was not the case.

"You're the perfect size! A woman came in today, I won't name names," Louisa began, although it was obvious it could easily be pried out of her. "She was teeny tiny as if she thought she was a girl. With crow's feet at the corners of her eyes, she wasn't fooling anybody as to her age. So thin that she looked as if she would break in two."

"I didn't know that was the fashion," Mrs. Burnside said, her forehead frowning.

"It isn't. I'm just saying that it doesn't look normal, and it didn't make her look any younger."

Simona came into the room and, greeting everyone, asked if there was anything she could get for them.

"No, thanks," Amanda said, pleased that the maid whom she had helped get the job was so attentive. "I think we'll have a tot of sherry, though."

Amanda had intended to do it herself, but Simona beat her to the punch. She went to the circular liquor cabinet and poured three small glasses, put them on a tray and passed them around.

"Thank you, my dear," Mrs. Burnside said. "She is a gem, Amanda," she added after the maid left the room.

They chatted about their day, anticipating the return of Mr. Burnside, when the telephone rang.

"I hope that's not your father saying he'll be detained," Mrs. Burnside said.

They waited for one of the maids to answer the call in the kitchen or the study and soon Simona returned.

"The call is for you, Miss," she said, looking at Amanda.

Once in her father's study, she picked up the instrument and, expecting it to be Brendan, leaned back in her father's chair for a long chat. It was he, but it was not a long conversation.

"I need your help," he said without preamble.

She sat upright. "What's the matter?" she asked, imagining something awful had happened to him.

"I'm at the home of one of your neighbors. Her husband has been killed and she is beyond hysterical, and I can't calm her down."

"Where is the staff?"

"Their afternoon off. She was home alone and when her husband hadn't come home from work, she went to the garage to see if his car was there. It was and that's when she discovered his body. Someone who had been walking his dog had already seen the body and called us. She is beside herself. I think having a woman present would help until we get things sorted out."

"Of course. Who is it, where is it?"

"It's Mrs. Hatton."

## Chapter 8

Without explaining to her mother and sister the circumstances, Amanda put on an overcoat and dashed to her car, driving it up the street and a few houses down to the Hatton residence. She could see Brendan's car out front, along with an ambulance and another police vehicle. But what struck her most was the eerie wailing of a woman that could be heard out in the street.

Amanda went to the front door, found it locked and rang the bell. Dominic Barone, one of the police detectives who worked for Brendan, let her in. The keening continued.

"It's chaos. We can't seem to calm her down to get any sort of coherent statement except that she went down to the garage and found his body."

"What happened?" Amanda imagined that he might have had a heart attack.

"He was shot."

Her eyes widened. "The poor woman." Almost immediately after that thought she wondered if it wasn't very convenient under the circumstances of Mrs. Hatton's wanting to dissolve the marriage before scolding herself for being so cynical. Or logical.

"It sounds like she is downstairs here somewhere?" Amanda asked. "Is the ambulance for her?"

"No, the ambulance is for her husband. She's in the study. We're trying to get her to calm down and Brendan has supplied her with a glass of whiskey, which has done nothing to reduce her agony. Or ours."

Although Amanda knew the family well, she had never been in their house before. However, it was laid out much like the other houses in Beacon Hill and she easily found the study with Brendan sitting next to Mrs. Hatton, who was howling with grief. As she approached, he looked up with a mixture of helplessness and relief.

"Mrs. Hatton. Mrs. Hatton!" Amanda repeated.

The woman stopped her vocalizations and stared at the newcomer.

"Who are you?" she asked, her voice hoarse. "You look familiar. Everyone is looking familiar lately."

Amanda sat down next to her at the table. "I'm Amanda Burnside. A neighbor. My sister is Louisa, who you've probably met."

"Oh."

"I've come to help you sort things out."

Mrs. Hatton stared at her, then at Brendan, and didn't seem to know what was going on.

"Where are your daughter and your son?"

"I don't know," she whispered. "They haven't come after them, too, have they?" She took a deep breath as if to start screaming again, but Amanda held the whiskey glass to her.

"Here, your throat must hurt. This will make it feel better."

Mrs. Hatton obeyed and took a large slug, wincing because, if anything, it made her throat hurt more. But the warmth of the liquid and the almost immediate effect momentarily relaxed her, although she still seemed disoriented. She relaxed her shoulders and out of one hand a pill bottle dropped to the ground.

"Mrs. Hatton! How many of these have you taken?"

"Just one. I think. I thought it would make the screaming stop."

Amanda held up the bottle for Brendan to see.

"You'd better put that whiskey away," he said to Amanda. "I've got to supervise downstairs. Dominic, you're in charge now."

Amanda looked at Dominic and motioned toward Mrs. Hatton with her eyes to signal that she was worried about the woman. Dominic shrugged.

"A doctor came with the ambulance. I'll just pop downstairs and have him come up and give his opinion if we should do something more. Like get her to the hospital to get her stomach pumped."

As soon as Dominic left, she could hear the distant sound of the front door opening and pounding footsteps as Kit came into the room, his overcoat flapping open and no hat on his head.

"Mother, Mother! Is she all right?" he asked Amanda since Mrs. Hatton's eyes were closed. "Why haven't they taken her to the hospital? Why is the ambulance still out front?"

He looked at Amanda with a glimmer of recognition and a look that said he had no idea why she should be in their house.

"Amanda Burnside," she reminded him. "I'm sitting with your mother while the police are downstairs."

"What? Why?"

Amanda was not pleased to have been put in the position of breaking the news to this young man whom she hadn't seen in several years and wouldn't have recognized except for his thick brown hair. "You'd better go down to the garage," she said. "I'll sit with your mother."

He blundered away toward the kitchen and the backstairs, almost colliding with the doctor on his way up. Kit was so confused by the scene that he didn't think to ask who this man with a medical bag was rushing up as he made his way down.

"What do you know?" the doctor asked Amanda.

"I've only just got here myself and she was given some whiskey in an attempt to calm her down. It was then that she dropped the pill bottle of what must be sedatives of some kind."

The doctor gave her a peeved look and looked at the label on the bottle. "How many of these has she had?"

"She said one, but I have no idea."

"How much alcohol has she had?"

"There's only been this one glass that I know of."

He seemed irritated at her and took a stethoscope out of his bag, listened to the woman's breathing and then took her pulse.

"Doctor, I'm a neighbor and was called in to help calm her down and keep her company. I've only been here a short time myself."

"I don't know if this is a murder and a suicide but it's a bloody mess down there."

Amanda immediately wondered if Mrs. Hatton would be considered the murderer and an attempted suicide—but that didn't make sense.

Amanda had fired weapons herself in the past and the last thing she could imagine was this petite woman holding a rifle up to her shoulder, or even a handgun, and killing her husband. What would be the point? She was on the brink of serving him with divorce papers.

"Is the weapon there?"

"That's not my interest. I was called to attend to Mr. Hatton and all I could do was pronounce him deceased. Now I am concerned about his wife and how many tablets she took."

More footsteps were heard approaching the dining room, and Doris came running in, still in her overcoat, stopping short when she saw Amanda and her inert mother and seeming not to be able to make sense of the scene.

"What's happened?"

"Your mother is indisposed."

"So, you called an ambulance?" she asked, looking at Amanda and the doctor. They, in turn, looked at each other; Amanda assumed the doctor would take the lead, which he eventually did. He stood up.

"I'm sorry, Miss Hatton, but you father is dead."

"What? Where?" She began to leave towards the sitting room where there were stairs to the bedrooms. The doctor grabbed at her coat.

"Please, Miss Hatton. Let me get the police and they can explain." He took his bag and went back to the kitchen and the garage, leaving the three women in the room. Luckily, Dominic had just come up the stairs and realized he once again had to deliver bad news.

Doris crumpled onto the floor. "That's not possible." She thought a few moments and asked, "Did he kill himself?"

"No, it doesn't appear so."

She looked at her mother, and Amanda could sense that Doris was turning over the possibilities in her mind: did her mother do this?

"Is Kit home yet?"

"He's downstairs with your father."

She got up to do the same, and Dominic took her arm. "I would caution you not to do that."

She pulled her arm away and went quickly off to the garage. Amanda looked around the study, a room much like the one in which her father spent time. Above one bookshelf was a picture of a group of young men posing for a formal portrait in front of a school building. Above the other was a composite picture of Skull and Bones members from Yale. Rather than being in a group photo, each undergraduate's picture was mounted in an orderly fashion within the frame. While she looked to see which one might be Mr. Hatton, she heard Doris scream as she evidently encountered the scene in the garage. Dominic sighed and left the room to bring the young people upstairs.

Once the ambulance had taken Mr. Hatton away and Kit and Doris returned to the study, their mother seemed to be more aware of what was going on. She took a deep breath and began to cry.

"How could this have happened? In our own home?"

Doris took off her coat and guided her mother into the sitting room, propped her up on the couch, covered her with a lap robe and sat next to her. Before Brendan and Dominic entered, Kit lit a fire, then sat in an armchair next to the fireplace.

"Is there anyone else in the house?" Brendan asked when he reappeared.

"It's their half-day off," Doris said. "None of the staff live in."

Dominic had a puzzled look on his face at hearing that.

"Times have changed," she explained. "And we can't afford as many staff as before and certainly not living space for them, too. In fact, we had to let the chauffeur go recently because of the expense."

Brendan's left eyebrow went up briefly at hearing that information, but he said nothing.

"I know this is a difficult time, but I have to ask you some preliminary questions." Since Mrs. Hatton was still groggy, he decided to start with the siblings. "Mr. Hatton, would you mind following me back to the dining room?"

Kit's eyebrows rose at the suggestion.

"We don't need to disturb your mother further," Brendan said.

"Don't worry, I'll stay," Doris said.

When they got to the dining room and were seated, Brendan began. "Mr. Hatton, where have you been today?"

"I woke late, had breakfast, pottered around and then had a late lunch with friends. And then a drink at my club." His tone was wounded as if anyone should suspect him.

"Did you return at any time?"

"No, you can ask…right, it was the staff's half day. But no, I was out and about most of the day."

"*Most* of the day?"

"All of the day until I got home just now."

Brendan was writing all this information down in his small notebook. After a pause, he resumed, "Did you and your father get along?"

"What kind of question is that?" Kit gave a bit of a laugh. "We got along as well as most fathers and sons do. He was always pushing me to do more, but I'm a college student. What does he expect? And after you graduate, your prospective employer doesn't ask what grade you got in history. All that matters is that you got that degree and are willing to work at whatever job it is you land."

"What field were you hoping to work in?" Brendan asked.

"Finance is still a bit of a bust so I thought I might try insurance or some corporate job."

Brendan wondered what a corporate job meant—applying to some big business to do what? Maybe with his background and connections, it didn't matter what.

"If that doesn't work out, law school is the next option."

Brendan was writing all that down and refraining from commenting on the young man's lack of direction.

"Can you supply us with the names of the people who you were with today? Just to make sure that we have all the details." Brendan smiled.

"Sure."

They looked at one another.

"You mean now?" Kit asked.

"Yes," Brendan answered and tore a sheet of paper from his notebook and handed it over.

Kit reached into the inner pocket of his suit and took out a fountain pen with his initials stamped onto the gold clip. He paused a moment while unscrewing the cap and then began to write a list of names that filled the page.

"I had lunch with these men," he said, bracketing the first three names. "Then went window shopping."

"Looking for anything in particular?" Brendan asked, thinking that was the oddest thing he had ever heard.

Women went window shopping; men went in a store and bought what they needed.

"I was looking for a thick sweater. Providence is damned cold in the winter." He looked down at his list of names. "These are the men who I met at the club although the porter would have logged my entrance."

"Does the porter also note when people step out for a moment or leave?"

Kit looked at Brendan as if he had arrived from a foreign country. "No, of course not. What an absurd question."

"What time did you leave your club?"

"About an hour ago. I walked for a while and then got a cab."

"You didn't drive in this morning?" Brendan asked.

Kit gave a bit of a laugh. "Yes, I did. But by the time I left the club, I'd forgotten where I parked the car. I'll remember in the morning."

"Let's hope you haven't racked up a stack of parking tickets in the meantime."

Kit smiled condescendingly at Brendan's mild concern. "Probably not."

"Is there anything else you can tell me about any enemies your father had or about his state of mind lately?"

"What are you suggesting? You don't think he killed himself, do you?"

"No, I was merely asking if there were any difficulties lately."

"Aside from the financial pressures—as everyone has been experiencing—no. Are we done here?"

"For the moment. Thank you, Mr. Hatton."

Kit stood up and went back to the sitting room, and Brendan couldn't help but note that his initial concern about his father seemed to have dissipated during the questioning as if it were an inconvenience.

Brendan followed him into the sitting room and caught Amanda's eyes, which were trying to communicate something to him. That would have to wait. "Miss Hatton?" He gestured toward the dining room, and she took a deep breath and squeezed her mother's hand.

"I know this is unpleasant, especially at this time, but it is important to get your recollections now when memory is fresh. Can you tell us your movements today?"

"I got up, pottered around. My father hadn't left for work yet and we all had breakfast together."

"Who is 'all'?"

"My mother and father and myself. Kit wasn't up yet."

"And then?"

"I had a luncheon with Amanda and the X-debs. A silly name we gave ourselves. We all had our coming out at the same time. Do you know what that means?"

"Yes, thank you, I do," Brendan answered with a straight face.

"We get together once a month at Valerie's club for lunch, a chat and gossip. In preparation, I took a bath and took my time choosing an outfit. Then I took a taxi and left with enough time to get there."

"Where were your parents?"

Doris seemed to freeze for a moment. "Daddy was still at home, as was my mother."

"Everything all right, there?"

"What do you mean?" she said, stiffening.

"Did you parents get along? Was everything all right? Shouldn't your father have gone to his office by then?"

"He usually would have, and I don't know why he hadn't. Things have been a bit topsy-turvy lately."

He was about to ask her to elaborate when they heard the doorbell ring and footsteps. Doris got up and looked back into the sitting room. "Oh, *him*" she said.

Brendan got up and saw a handsome young man rush over to Mrs. Hatton.

"Who's that?"

Doris exhaled with annoyance. "Mr. Van Eaton."

## Chapter 9

Brendan recognized the name from conversations with Amanda and wondered how he had heard the news about Mr. Hatton so soon. The look of concern on the young man's face could have been genuine regret for the family, but Brendan wondered if the loss of income from the now moot divorce case wasn't more of an issue.

"Unless you need to speak to him…." Brendan trailed off.

"No," Doris said, and they both sat down.

"What did you mean by topsy-turvy?"

Brendan could see she regretted having said that and she looked down in her lap.

"In what way?" he persisted, with a smile on his face.

"Things have been difficult since the Crash. And Kit seems to be taking longer than four years to get through college."

"Why is that?"

"You'll have to ask him."

"Lunches with the boys? Cocktails with friends?"

"I wouldn't know," Doris said, although it was obvious that she had some inkling.

"Did you get along with your father?"

"Yes!" she answered with vigor. "He was the best father. I can't imagine how this has happened to him. He didn't have any enemies—he was so very well-liked and respected."

"It might have been an attempted robbery," Brendan suggested.

"I'm sure it was. People think everyone in Beacon Hill is a millionaire. We've often seen unsavory people loitering behind the house. We always keep the doors locked and the staff are very careful about letting just anybody in."

"Except the staff were not here this afternoon," Brendan said. He looked up through his dark lashes at her.

"That's right. If it had been any other day, this might not have happened."

"Or maybe someone knew that the staff would not be here and took advantage of that knowledge. Do you know if your father was coming in or going out?" Brendan thought he should have put his hand on the hood earlier to check if it was warm.

"Oh! I have no idea."

"Your mother will know. I'll ask her."

"Please take great care with my mother. She is in a fragile state just now."

"Of course. I'm aware that she is. But back to you, after your luncheon, what did you do the rest of the afternoon?"

Doris looked down at her hands again and frowned for a moment. "You may think this is odd, but I went to the Museum of Fine Arts."

"Why should I think that was odd? Because a police detective couldn't be interested in art?" He refrained from adding the other qualifier, 'Irish.'

She blushed deeply but said nothing.

"How long would you say you were there?"

"From about two-thirty until I came home. You saw me come in."

"Yes," he said. He looked back over his notes and then added, "Can you think of anyone with a motive to kill your father?"

"No! Now let me get back to my mother." She got up abruptly and left the room.

Brendan followed, intending to talk to Mrs. Hatton, who had calmed down considerably since he first arrived. Van Eaton had one of her hands in his while Kit and Doris gave him sour looks. Amanda sat on the other side of Mrs. Hatton and looked from Brendan to Van Eaton, trying to signal to him. Brendan nodded at her and then approached the group.

"I'm sorry, Mrs. Hatton, but I do need to ask you some questions."

The attorney stood up. "I don't think that's a good idea just now."

"And who are you?" Brendan asked.

"I'm a friend. Hugh Van Eaton." He paused and looked at the siblings as if to phrase the next sentence carefully. "I've worked with the family."

Kit exploded. "What? Dad never mentioned you."

"It was your mother I was assisting. To do with some issues with her own family. I'm afraid I can't say more at the moment."

Kit and Doris looked at each other and then at their mother.

Mrs. Hatton waved her hand. "To do with an inheritance from your grandparents," she said.

Brendan assumed that if she could make up that explanation so quickly, she was alert enough to answer his questions.

"Mrs. Hatton, can you tell me about your husband's movements today?"

"He went to his office downtown mid-morning, and I didn't expect him back until dinner."

"Did he tell you if he was going to meet anyone? Did he telephone home at any time?"

"No, it was just a regular morning." She looked at Van Eaton, who nodded his head.

"What were your movements today?"

"I took my time getting ready this morning. The staff left just before noon, and I looked at the mail and wrote a few letters." She pursed her lips in thought. "I had the lunch that Cook had left for me, then made up the menus for the week. Then I went into the study and read for a while and feeling tired, went upstairs and took a nap."

"And then?"

"I confess I slept longer than I intended." She stopped speaking.

"When did you think to look for your husband?"

She breathed in and out and Van Eaton squeezed her hand in encouragement. "I'm not sure. It was dark outside, and I went to the garage and saw the door was open. I expected that he might be going to close the door but not hearing anything, I called out to him and walked toward the back of the car and found him." She stopped abruptly. "I must have screamed because I heard a dog barking in the distance."

"It must have been the man who called us to tell us of seeing your husband. He identified himself as Mr. Daugherty," Dominic said. "He had been walking his dog and took his dog home before he called."

After a pause, Brendan asked, "Are there any guns in the house?"

"Yes," Kit said.

"Show me," Brendan said, getting up.

He followed Kit to the study where the young man said, "My father keeps them locked in the closet there." He went to the desk first and rooted around for the key, then opened the door. "We used to do a bit of hunting."

After the door was unlocked, he pulled the chain to turn on the overhead bulb. Brendan looked over his shoulder.

"It's gone!"

"What?"

"The Winchester 1876!" He pushed several other gun cases out of the way. "It's been stolen. Do you think that was the weapon that killed my father?"

"I can't say for sure. We'll know more after an autopsy."

"You don't have to do that, do you?" Doris asked, suddenly at her brother's shoulder.

Kit responded, "They have to in these cases."

They made their way back into the sitting room and Kit delivered the news to his mother.

"Do you have any idea the last time your husband or anyone else had been in that closet?"

Mrs. Hatton looked perplexed. "There are other things stored in that closet, so I couldn't be sure."

"You were in the study this afternoon, isn't that correct?" Brendan asked.

"See here!" Van Eaton shouted as he stood up quickly.

"I need to ask all the questions that are pertinent. You should know that sir. Have you ever been in this house before?"

Van Eaton's face froze for a moment, and he didn't speak.

"Yes, he has," Doris said, glaring at him.

"Mrs. Hatton, we'll need to talk to your staff tomorrow and get more information. Would ten o'clock suit?"

After they had left the Hatton residence, Brendan leaned over to Amanda and asked if he could stop by her house and use the facilities.

She looked at him. "Facilities? You mean a bathroom?"

"Yes," he responded and Dominic, who stood nearby, sniggered. "You don't expect me to use the bathroom in the murdered man's house, do you?"

"You never know what you'll find in the medicine cabinet," Dominic responded. "It looks to me like the wife has an assortment of things to soothe the psyche."

"Come on with me," Brendan said to Dominic, who had driven them both to Beacon Hill. "We may get a drink out of this, too."

It was only a few blocks to the Burnside residence and, once inside, the three appreciated the warmth of the house. Hearing their approach, Simona opened the door, wondering why the police were at the house.

"Business," Amanda said to her questioning look. She directed Brendan to the guest restroom down the hall and asked Dominic if he needed to use it. He declined and looked around at her home, impressed by the size and the old money look of the place.

Simona offered to take his overcoat, but he protested that they wouldn't be staying long.

"Let's have a drink," Amanda suggested and took him into the sitting room where her parents sat near the fire, her father absorbed in the evening newspaper and her mother doing needlepoint.

"Mother, Daddy, this is Dominic Barone, who works with Brendan. They've just come from the Hattons' house where the unfortunate Mr. Hatton has met his death."

Mrs. Burnside predictably clutched at her bosom and Mr. Burnside put the newspaper down.

"How awful," her father said. "But why did you need to be there?"

"Dominic, please sit down. Daddy, could you provide a tot of sherry? Brendan called me because Mrs. Hatton was hysterical, and he thought that the presence of a woman would calm her down."

Her father stood at the drinks cabinet and turned around. "Where was everyone else? Her children? The staff?"

"Half day for the staff with Kit and Doris out and about. She was all alone in the house."

Mrs. Burnside gave a whimper of commiseration. "The poor woman."

Brendan reappeared and nodded his thanks to Amanda while Mr. Burnside got three glasses, one for Amanda and one for each of the detectives.

"Thank you, sir," the men said.

"I'm sure you can't discuss the case yet, but I hope it wasn't some burglary gone wrong," Mr. Burnside said.

"Of course, it's too early to tell."

"Mr. Van Eaton showed up while we were there," Amanda said.

Her father looked at her and at Brendan.

"Who's that?" Mrs. Burnside asked.

"One of our younger staff," he answered. Amanda noted that he didn't describe him as a colleague.

"He said he had been representing Mrs. Hatton with some issues relating to her parents' estate. He had evidently been to the house before," Amanda said.

"I didn't know attorneys made house calls," Brendan said with a straight face.

"They don't, unless the client is incapacitated," Mr. Burnside replied.

"Don't talk business, dear. I know Amanda has missed her dinner and I imagine you have, as well."

The two detectives got up simultaneously, thanking their host for the drink and made to leave.

"No, you don't," Amanda said. "Come into the kitchen and we'll make you a roast pork sandwich."

They tried to decline, but she was adamant. "I'm starving and I'm sure you must be, too." She took Brendan by the hand and led him through to the kitchen, with Dominic in tow. "Take off your coats at least," she added.

"Your parents will think I'm a barbarian, barging in, using the restroom and then eating all your food."

"I said I would make us sandwiches, not give you all there was to eat in the house."

Cook had already left for the evening, but Amanda managed to find the roast in the refrigerator and gave Brendan the job of carving thin slices of meat.

"Here is mustard, butter and mayonnaise. I'll slice some tomatoes. What else?"

"Coffee would be good," Brendan said. "We'll be working late tonight sorting through what we know so far."

Amanda went about preparing coffee, which she had only recently learned to make. While the water was boiling, she said, "Don't you think it's significant that nobody was in the house except Mrs. Hatton, who took a long nap?"

"We'll be back out tomorrow to talk to the staff."

"Anyone could have taken that gun out of the closet and shot him. From what you said, the key was hardly in a secret location," Amanda said as she put plates out.

"We don't know if the missing gun was the one used on Mr. Hatton. It could have been missing for some time, for all we know."

"We didn't ask the last time that anyone saw it," Dominic said.

The men had sliced the bread on the butcher block central workspace, put it on plates and then each spread the condiment of choice on before adding the meat and the sliced tomatoes.

"Oh, this is good," Dominic said after a large bite.

"We really shouldn't be discussing this case with a civilian," Brendan said.

"I'm hardly that. You were the one who called to have me go over to the Hattons' to assist."

"Well, just to calm her down, that's all."

"Oh, no—you're not going to pull that on me. I'm either in or I'm out."

Brendan stopped mid-bite. "Coffee's percolating."

Amanda turned back to the stove and let a few minutes go by before turning off the gas and returning with cups and saucers, sugar and milk.

"Come, sit down," Brendan said, trying to appease her. "I'll pour."

"Actually, I know more about this case than you do," Amanda said.

"Oh, really?"

"Not only have I been friends with Doris for a long time, but I know things about her family. I could call you at the station and relay what I know, but the switchboard will be closed at this hour. If you call me, I'll see what I can share with you. I must consult with my counsel."

"Who's that?" Dominic asked, puzzled by the exchange.

"Edward Burnside, Esquire."

After the two men left, Amanda did a perfunctory cleanup by putting the food away and leaving the dishes unwashed in the sink for Cook to deal with in the morning because she had more pressing matters. Returning to the sitting room, she asked her father if they could have a confidential chat.

Mrs. Burnside looked up from her needlework. "Is something the matter that I should know about?" she asked.

"It's a business thing," Amanda said.

"I can just as well get ready for bed. There's a wonderful mystery I'm reading. By the time I'm done, I may be able to help you solve one of yours! Goodnight."

Amanda took her shoes off and made herself comfortable on the sofa by curling her feet beneath her. "It's about Hugh Van Eaton," she said.

"I thought so," her father replied.

"He knows all the details of Mrs. Hatton's marriage and Mr. Hatton's activities. And I can't help but wonder if he might have been taking advantage of that knowledge."

"In what way?"

"By playing on her feelings for one. I could tell from your response earlier this evening that you thought it odd that he should be visiting Mrs. Hatton in her home more than once. What you didn't see was the excessive attention he paid her when he appeared this evening. Holding her hand, squeezing it, and her rapt looks at him."

Mr. Burnside made a slight growling noise.

"Doris and Kit seemed to have been aware that he was a regular visitor but were not aware of the vague family business to which he referred. I'm sure that Brendan picked up on the undercurrents, but he isn't aware that a divorce was imminent. What I wanted to ask you is whether I can share some of the details that I know."

"Such as?"

"That Mrs. Hatton was planning a divorce, for one. That seems very important."

"I should think that would be all right. It is pertinent and it could explain why Van Eaton had been to the house."

"He suggested that she had retained him for some work concerning her parents' estate. I don't know if that's true. It may be the case, but I suspect it was his way of covering his real purpose in meeting with her. Meaning the divorce, of course," she added.

"Not a budding relationship?"

"I don't know if it was budding or full-blown."

"In any case, he's in over his head," Mr. Burnside said. "I may need to talk to the partners about pulling him off representation of Mrs. Hatton. I don't like how this is beginning to look. After all, a divorce is moot at this point."

They were both lost in thought for a few moments.

"It's curious to weigh the advantages of being a widow versus a divorcée," Amanda said.

"Well put, my dear. If Mr. Hatton followed the usual custom, his widow has likely inherited the entire estate. Unless he has set aside significant sums for his two children."

"And there are reasons to suspect he might have a financial obligation to someone else."

Mr. Burnside looked up. "You have been discreet. There may be debts that would need to be settled from his estate as well."

"I don't know if the house was his, hers or theirs or whether he had other property. That wasn't part of Gilbert's research."

"Without knowing the extent of the estate and ownership issues, it is impossible to say whether Mrs. Hatton would benefit financially from his death. In my opinion, from what facts we know, she certainly will have more sympathy as a widow and not lose face in her social circle. That counts for a lot. You have my permission to share what information you think pertinent with Brendan and the Boston Police Department."

Amanda thanked her father, slipped her shoes back on and was about to ascend the stairs to her room when the telephone rang. It was Brendan.

"I hope you're sitting down," she said. "I have a lot to tell you."

## Chapter 10

Bleary eyed from a long night reviewing case notes with Dominic, Brendan shuffled to the kitchen in his apartment and began the ritual of making coffee. He faced a long morning of talking to the Hattons' staff, hoping they had some relevant information, but more to the point, were willing to share it. It always surprised him that, even when working conditions weren't the best and salary was minimal, many servants continued to be protective of their employers.

Brendan stopped at the bakery near the station and bought a sticky bun to go. With another cup of coffee at work, he felt prepared to face the world. Hearing a rustle, he looked up to see the Chief standing in the doorway.

"Top of the morning," he said. He came in and sat in the chair opposite Brendan and crossed his legs ankle over knee. "We've got a visitor from the Midwest coming this week. A fella who has studied how they do police and detective work in Europe. Stayed about a month between England and France."

"Sounds like a difficult assignment."

The Chief chuckled. "And now that Chicago is snowed in, he's coming east to visit us."

"To take notes?"

"Partly that and partly to tell us what he discovered in his travels. From the first information, it seems our European cousins require more education before hiring onto the force. At least a high school diploma, which is not a bad thing. It narrows down the possible hires, however. The Chief in Chicago told me that they have more lab technicians and a more scientific way of analyzing crime scenes."

"We should be open to any good suggestions."

"Agreed." The Chief looked around the room and stood. "I understand you're on the Hatton case."

Brendan stood as well. "Just got it last night. Lots to do. Has someone inquired about it?"

"Let's just say the Mayor would like kid gloves on this one."

Brendan wondered what an upper-crust Bostonian had in common with an Irish American Mayor but kept his questions to himself.

"Remember, 'Yours is not to question why. Yours is but to do or die.'" He winked and left the room.

Brendan sat and muttered to himself, "That's not the quote. It's '*Theirs* is not to question why. *Theirs* is but to do *and* die.' And Tennyson was referring to the blunder of the Light Brigade charging into the valley of Death." He shuddered at the analogy.

Dominic popped in shortly thereafter wearing his overcoat.

"Aren't we going to the Hatton place again?"

"As soon as I finish this," Brendan answered, pointing to what remained of his breakfast. "You look as bad as I feel," he commented, observing the dark circles under Dominic's eyes.

"Someone in the neighborhood has a yowling cat. It's probably like that in their house, which is why they toss it into the yard to share the joy with the rest of us."

"You could have let it into your place."

"Sure. I need a cat like a hole in the head. Maybe if we're nice to the Hattons' staff, they'll give us coffee."

Brendan looked up through his lashes. "I wouldn't count on it. People with money are often surprisingly stingy."

"Then let me grab a cup here before we go," Dominic said, disappearing.

Half an hour later, they were in their usual, unmarked car driving up to Beacon Hill.

"Amanda is working for her father's firm doing a cleanup of the former investigator's files. One of those files involved Mr. Hatton."

"Oh, yeah?"

"Mrs. Hatton was seeking a divorce although he didn't know it yet, from what I've learned. Amanda gave me some other details of his interesting life." He looked over at Dominic. "We've got a lot of people to talk to."

"Popular, was he?"

"That's one way of putting it."

They pulled up out front and Brendan rang the doorbell. It took another attempt before a woman in a maid's uniform came to the door.

"Yes?" she asked.

They showed their badges, and she let them in with a cold look. "Who shall I call?"

"If you don't mind, we'd like to talk to the cook."

There was a look of surprise, and she ushered them into the kitchen, a carbon copy of the Burnsides', occupied by a similarly stout, middle-aged woman; however, this one lacked the warmth and charm of the other. She didn't greet them when the maid ushered them in and announced them but gave them a look of disdain and continued her work of mixing dough in a large bowl.

"Good morning," Brendan ventured.

"Nothing good about this morning," she responded, pounding it down.

"It's a sad day for the family and I'm sorry that I have to ask you some questions."

"I stay in the kitchen the entire day. Except sometimes I go out to have a cigarette and get a bit of fresh air."

That seemed contradictory to Brendan, although he didn't comment.

"What I mean is, I do not mingle with the family. The Missus comes in here once a week and hands me the menus for the next seven days. I can tell her whether something might not be available at the markets, and she makes adjustments. I do the ordering through the butcher and all the rest of them, but I'm in here all day. After dinner is served, I go home. That's my day."

"May I sit down?" Brendan asked, needing to write in his notebook. He looked around and saw a plate of pastries and surmised that they weren't going to be on offer.

"If you like," she answered.

He pulled out a stool and sat down.

"Do you feed the rest of the staff?" Brendan asked.

"What there's left of the staff," she sniffed. "They get lunch and that's it. None of them live in."

"Have some people left recently?"

"The butler was let go a few weeks ago. The chauffeur got sacked just last week and Mr. Hatton drives himself. What Mrs. Hatton is going to do now, who knows? She doesn't know how to drive."

"Was there any reason?"

She stopped what she was doing and gave him a withering look. "I'll say. Lack of money. Like everyone else these days." She plopped the dough onto the countertop and began kneading it. Brendan admired her skill and her arm muscles evident with the rolled-up sleeves.

"So, there is you, and who else?"

"Two. Sally let you in and June is floating around somewhere. The heavy cleaning is done by some outside folks, yardwork, too."

Brendan was writing this down when the swinging door from the dining room opened, and Mrs. Hatton stood still at the sight of the detectives. All she said was, "Oh."

"Do you need me for something, Ma'am?" the cook asked.

"I did, but now I've forgotten what it was."

Brendan stood up. "We were just getting some background on everyone's job and whereabouts yesterday."

"You haven't asked me that yet," the cook said.

"Well then, where were you yesterday?"

"Half day off. Went back home. I live with my son and daughter-in-law. Put my feet up after a long week's work."

Mrs. Hatton's cheeks flushed at the comment.

"As long as you're here, may we have a space to interview the two maids? Sally and June?"

"Certainly. You can use the dining room if that suits," Mrs. Hatton said.

"That would be fine, thank you," Brendan said, and Mrs. Hatton left quickly. "Where can I find June and Sally?" he asked the cook.

She shrugged. "Beats me. I'm here in the kitchen all day."

"Thank you for your time," Brendan said.

As they entered the empty dining room, he wondered if he was supposed to roam around the house looking for them. Then, as a random thought, he also wondered why the cook referred to Mrs. Hatton as 'Missus' but addressed her as 'Ma'am.'"

He stood idly for a few minutes and was pleased to see that Mrs. Hatton had taken the hint and produced the maid whom he hadn't met, introduced as June. She was young and wide-eyed, but before they sat down, they assured her they just needed some information. Mrs. Hatton left the room.

"How long have you been working here?"

"Just two years. My dad lost his job when the Crash happened and all of us kids had to leave school and get work. Someone at our church got me the position here. Neither me nor my family have ever been in service," she added.

"The Crash changed a lot of lives," Brendan agreed, looking at the young woman who might have been a teenager, although she wore her hair up and attempted to be older than she looked.

"Where were you yesterday?"

"I came in early, as usual. I did the bedrooms. Made the beds, picked up the dirty clothes, tidied the bathrooms and came back downstairs to help clear the table."

"Was all the family at breakfast?"

"Oh, yes. Young Mr. Hatton came down later than the rest, as he usually does when he's at home. He's away at college, you know." She said this as a point of pride.

"Handsome young man," Brendan observed.

She colored immediately. "Yes, he is."

"Was there any conversation at the breakfast table? Such as who was going where or who was going to do what?"

"Not that I heard. I only did the clearing. But I understand they don't usually talk much at breakfast. It looks like Mr.

Hatton reads the paper and the others just eat." She gave a bit of a giggle.

"That's funny," Brendan said. "I come from a big family, and you're lucky to get a word in edgewise."

"Me, too," she said with a smile.

"Did the family get along, though?"

She hesitated. "I suppose. They didn't seem to talk much or do things together. Everyone seemed to go their own way."

"Interesting," Brendan said as he wrote. He looked up and saw her concerned look, so incongruous on her childish face. "Don't worry; I won't be telling the family where any of this information came from."

"That's good. Because I do need this job." She pressed her lips together as if to will them to be careful.

"What time did you leave yesterday?"

"We worked until noon and left right after. It's one of the few days to do any of our own personal business. That and Sunday afternoon, but almost everything is closed then, of course."

"What did you do yesterday?"

"I went to the bank to deposit some of my wages. The rest goes to my parents, of course." She lowered her voice. "I stopped into the Employment Exchange—please don't mention this to Mrs. Hatton. I wanted to see if there was something on offer that paid better than here. I took my mother for a doctor's visit and then just stayed at home helping with the chores there."

"Were you aware of any tensions in the house here? Among the family or the staff and the family?"

June gave his question some thought before answering. "They let the butler go a few weeks ago, which was a bit of a shock."

"How so?"

"It wasn't as if he was doing a bad job. I got the impression that the family needed to economize. He was torn up about it. And of course, then we all were wondering who would be next."

"That's tough."

"And then just last week, they let Joe go."

"Who's that?"

"Joe Epperson. He was the chauffeur. They said they had to economize further."

"How did he take it?"

"Well, it was a total shock. He had no idea it was coming. None of us did. He was not pleased that they only gave him a week's extra wages to 'soften the blow,' as he said they put it." She leaned in closer to add in a whisper, "He and Sally were stepping out and she was furious. But she had to hold her tongue—she didn't want to get the sack, too."

"This is a big house to run with just the three of you," Brendan observed.

"Mrs. Hatton has someone come in twice a month to do the heavy cleaning, and we're meant to keep up on the dusting and such in between times. Cook let slip that it wasn't too long before I got here that they had a housekeeper, too."

"That's a big household," Brendan said.

"The housekeeper left of her own accord, so naturally most of what she did got divided among the rest of the staff."

*With no extra pay*, Brendan thought.

"I know it's been hard for everybody these days, but still…."

He nodded. "I only have one other question for you. Well, it's kind of a long one. How do you divide up your work, you and Sally? Do you do certain rooms, and she does others?"

"What a funny question," June smiled. "I suppose back when they had a housekeeper, she would have assigned the duties each day. You're right, though. I do the upstairs and Sally does the downstairs rooms because she was here before me. I do the bedrooms, tidy the clothes off the floor." At this she gave Brendan a look that conveyed her opinion of people who would toss their clothing on the floor. "Brief swipes of the bathrooms, if everyone is up and about, that is." Another look suggesting somebody usually slept in. "While Sally's job is somewhat easier, it stuck her with answering the door because there was no butler to do it and it interrupts whatever chore she is doing, such as polishing the silver, for example."

"I hate it when people interrupt my polishing of the family silver," Brendan said, which elicited a giggle from June.

"We're pretty busy most of the time."

"Was the study one of the rooms that she did?"

"Yes. But only if Mr. Hatton wasn't using it. She had to open the drapes, dust, but not move any of the papers on the desk."

Brendan looked over his notes and debated whether to ask the next question. "Were you aware there were guns in the house?"

Her eyebrows raised. "No."

"You never heard anybody talking about guns or hunting? Or where they may have been kept?"

"No. Absolutely not." She looked at him for a few moments. "Somebody told me Mr. Hatton had been shot. Is that why you are asking me?"

"Yes, he was shot, but I was just curious as to what you had observed or heard."

"Nothing." She was adamant. "I swear," she said, holding up her hand.

## Chapter 11

While Brendan was at the Hatton house talking to the staff, Dominic was tracking down the helpful neighbor who had called the police the day before. He had the man's telephone number and address and found his house just a few blocks away.

Dominic called from the station before they left that morning, indicating his intention to stop by, and anticipated that Mr. Daugherty would answer the bell immediately. After another ring, a young man answered the door and told him to try the entry in the back. A bit put out at being directed to the servants' entrance, Dominic made his way along an icy path beneath pine trees and saw a door with the man's name on it. There was a brass knocker and he rapped it.

A middle-aged man with fading red hair and a moustache to match opened the door with a smile. He had hardly said anything before the head of an Irish setter poked though the gap and the man had to call the dog back inside.

"Hector! Back inside," he said as he grabbed hold of the collar. "He won't bite," he added, opening the door fully for Dominic to enter. He let go of the dog, which sniffed the detective's shoes and lower pant legs intently.

"Needs to know where you've been. Come in, sit down, please."

Dominic looked around at the small living room, a newspaper on the couch and an armchair facing it.

"I'm sorry. I was confused and went to the big house that faces the street."

"That's my house. I rent it out and live back here. It's smaller, of course, but then I don't have to take care of all those rooms. It's cozy and all the space Hector and I need." He gestured to the armchair and Dominic slipped off his overcoat and sat down.

"I need to follow up about the incident involving Mr. Hatton."

"Dreadful," Mr. Daugherty said. His mouth turned down and he shook his head.

"I know you talked to someone else at our station, but could you tell me more about what happened on Tuesday? First, how did you happen to be behind the Hattons' house?"

"I walk my dog twice a day, in the early morning and the late afternoon. I try to change the route every few days to give him variety." The dog had sat at his feet and was getting his head petted and looking up at his owner. "I went onto the street in front of my house, took a left and then went into the alleys behind the houses on my way back here. I could see the garage door open, and Cromwell stopped, which wasn't unusual; he's a curious fellow. Since he had stopped, I thought it only courteous for me to say hello even though I didn't know the Hattons well. The driver's side door was open and as I moved closer, I saw a body on the ground. Poor fellow," Daugherty said, and Dominic thought he was referring to Mr. Hatton but soon found out he meant the dog.

"Scared him terribly. Scent of blood, I suppose. It made him bark wildly. I looked around and called out but he didn't move and there was no one else there. I thought I might enter the garage and go up the back stairs to tell someone. And then I realized I would frighten the servants, so we raced home, and I called from here, agreeing to come back to the scene in order to make a statement if needed."

"Good thinking. Did you see anyone in the alley?"

"No. There's usually nobody about unless someone is emptying trash or backing their car out."

"Any strangers on the street while you were walking the dog?"

"No, it was quiet. It was dark and the wind was picking up. No time to be out and about."

"Did you hear anything prior to walking down the alley?"

"Such as?"

"A gunshot, for example."

"Certainly not."

"Do you own a gun?"

"I own several, but they are up in the big house. Locked up in the attic."

"Are you sure they are still there?"

"Say, what is this? Are you suggesting that I had something to do with this?" His abrupt change of tone made the dog get off his haunches, fully alert.

"Not at all. Who rents your house?"

"Four young men."

Dominic looked up at Daugherty, thinking that sounded odd.

"Is it a social group or a fraternity?"

"No, no. These are all graduates of Brown, my alma mater. They are young men starting out in business and wanting to spread their wings a bit. I either know their families or, in the case of one, made sure he had impeccable references. I was very clear in the contract that there were to be no parties and no young women spending the night."

Dominic wrote this down and asked, "How sure are you that they abide by the rules?"

Daugherty held up his index finger and said with a smile, "I have a spy. The woman who cleans the big house cleans here, too. She tells me everything that goes on, down to who left dishes in the sink."

"Does she do bed checks, too?"

"Certainly not. That would be intrusive."

"I was joking," Dominic said.

"I've been assured these are men of integrity and, if they promised they would abide by the requirements of living there, they would honor that."

Four young bachelors in a big house without supervision? Dominic kept his reservations to himself.

"Is there anything else you can tell me?"

"I'm afraid not."

"Could you give me the names of the tenants? Perhaps they heard something."

"I doubt it. They were probably all at work."

"Good point, but just in case."

Daugherty got up and went to a small desk in the corner and took a paper out of a drawer. "Here," he said, handing over the rental contract that had been written in longhand.

Dominic was about to fold it to put in his pocket when the man stopped him.

"That's an original. Just write down the names, please."

The detective did so, as well as the addresses of their previous residences that the young men had provided.

"Thank you for your time. And you might want to check on those guns in the attic."

Dominic walked back to the Hattons' house, looking up around himself in the alley, wondering if anyone else could have heard a gunshot, but he could hardly see any houses through the dense pine trees. Still, it seemed strange that no one had come forward with more information.

He went up the back steps to the kitchen door, knocked and, seeing the cook look up, walked in. She didn't say a word to him, just jerked her head in the direction of the swinging door that led to the dining room where Brendan was interviewing the other maid, Sally, who looked none too pleased. She was older than June and likely concerned that the death of Mr. Hatton would alter her employment status.

"Hey, Dominic. We were just starting."

Dominic took off his hat in a sort of greeting, to which she closed her eyes and turned her head away,

"I can't imagine what you think I could possibly know about the family's affairs," she said.

"You've worked here for several years. I imagine that, except for the cook, you probably know a lot about their affairs."

She gave him a puzzled look.

"The cook says she never gets out of the kitchen."

"Ha! She stays through breakfast, lunch and dinner and hears everything that they discuss."

"June said they were very quiet during meals."

"Oh, did she? Just protecting her job, is what. They had some harsh words for one another when they weren't giving each other the silent treatment."

"What about?"

"Mr. Hatton thought his son was a layabout and his daughter would never get married."

"You heard him say that?"

"I certainly did." She nodded her head for emphasis, making the pinned-up curls at the side of her head jiggle.

"How did Mrs. Hatton react?"

She scoffed. "She never said anything to counter him. She stayed quiet."

"Did you ever hear them arguing?"

"Not me. My job is mostly downstairs, and it seems they kept a civil tone in the more public rooms. But I could hear arguing upstairs from time to time. No matter what June says."

Brendan continued to write in his notebook and would discuss this discrepancy with Dominic later when they were back at the station.

"I understand the butler was let go a while ago."

Sally gave a derisive sniff. "Thought he was so posh. All he did was read the newspaper and answer the door. Some job. Except since then, I'm the one who has to answer the bell and I don't get to sit around reading the paper. For my old salary, if you can believe it!"

"Oh, I can," Brendan said, and it was the first time she seemed to relax. "Working folks get the short end of the stick all the time. And the chauffeur was also let go?"

Sally stiffened up again. "Yes, just last week. Same excuse: they had to economize."

Brendan turned a few pages back and read out, "Joe Epperson?"

"That's right."

"Were you particularly friendly with Joe?"

Her eyes went to slits as she stared at him. "What little birdie has been talking to you?"

Brendan didn't answer her question.

"Listen, we were saving up to get married and now that's on hold. He's done being in service, but jobs are scarce, in case you hadn't noticed. Don't you worry, he'll land on his feet. And he had nothing to do with Mr. Hatton's death. He was out with me that afternoon. We went to the pictures."

"What did you see?" Brendan asked calmly.

"The double feature. On Tremont Street."

"I don't suppose you have the ticket stub."

"Don't be ridiculous. Do I look like the type who has time for putting stuff in a scrapbook? Are we done here?"

"Sure. We can be done for now. But I'll need to talk to Joe."

"Do what you have to do. But he's clean. Of this place and that murder."

She got up abruptly, glared at Brendan and left the room.

BASED on what Amanda had told him about the divorce case, Brendan knew he had to interview the two women whom Gilbert had observed Hatton visiting. The first person on his list was Florence Dodge, identified as his secretary. He went to her address, assuming he would find her at home and in mourning, but his knocks on her apartment door went unanswered. A neighbor in a housedress peeked out the door at the noise, and Brendan caught her attention. She looked startled at having been seen and could offer no information other than she rarely saw Miss Dodge, who worked during the day and didn't socialize with the neighbors. Brendan left his card under the door and left.

Next, he went to the Gisriels' apartment on Commonwealth, a quiet, five-story brick building. He soon realized the reason for the silence was that these were all working people, and no one was at home. This was confirmed when he buzzed at the Gisriels' apartment and got no answer. He continued down the hall buzzing and knocking without any response and decided he had wasted his time. Amanda had told him that they worked at Monsieur Josef's salon, but he was hesitant to jeopardize their employment by talking to them there. Instead, he called the salon, asked to speak to Louisa and, without explaining his rationale, asked her to get Marigold to the phone. She sounded very young and puzzled.

"I'm sorry to call you at work, but this is Chief Inspector Halloran and I need to talk to you about the death of Mr. Hatton."

He heard a gasp. "I didn't know he had died," she said.

"It was yesterday. Perhaps you haven't seen the newspapers."

"No."

"I need to talk to you and your mother. Could you meet me at the diner—luncheonette down the street from the salon? In about thirty minutes?"

"Yes, I'll tell my mother."

Brendan was already seated in a booth when he saw the mother and daughter cross the street, arm in arm, if not for companionship, then for support. They entered, looked around and he waved to them. They didn't smile or have any facial expression as they came and stood by the booth.

"Please, sit down."

The daughter slid into the banquette, her mother following, both holding their handbags in their laps and keeping their faces deliberately neutral.

"Why have you called us?" the mother asked with a strong accent, her face drawn with worry. "Is this about an immigration status?"

That hadn't occurred to Brendan as being a possible issue. "No, the city police don't enforce that. Won't you have some coffee?"

The women looked at each other and nodded to him.

He thought he might make some chit-chat to warm up the atmosphere and soon realized that nothing he could say or do would cut the tension. After ordering three coffees, he took a breath and began.

"We know that Mr. Hatton was a frequent visitor at your home. Why was that?"

Mrs. Gisriel answered. "Mr. Hatton was someone I met when I first came to this country." She stopped as if that was enough information.

"Here, in Boston?"

"I met him in New York. He had some connection with resettlement organizations."

"Which ones?"

"I can't remember the name. It was a long time ago."

"During the war?" he asked, stopping when the waitress delivered the coffee.

The two women made a long business of adding cream and sugar, stirring and tasting.

"After the war."

"I didn't realize Mr. Hatton had worked in New York."

"He did at that time. He had been invalided out of the service," Mrs. Gisriel said.

"And I didn't realize he had served. What sort of assistance did the organization provide?"

"I had come from Alsace, the area that Germany and France were always arguing about and there were few Alsatians—no group to assist, and I felt quite alone."

"There still aren't," Marigold said.

"The organization found me a place to live and connected me to the several couturiers in New York, where I found work."

"That seems to have worked out well," Brendan said.

"Yes. The kind of work I do was much in demand."

"When did you move to Boston?"

"About three years ago. Despite the economic situation, New York was getting too expensive, and I had to travel so far to get to and from work. Monsieur Josef had seen some of my handiwork at a fashion show and inquired, 'Who does your beading?' That was me, of course. And he wrote and asked if I would come to Boston to work in his atelier. I wasn't sure about making such a big move, but he offered me more than I made in New York and Mari had finished school, so I proposed that we both work for him. It is not so expensive/ living here." She gave a small smile.

"Where is Mari's father?"

"He died in the war." She crossed herself after she said that.

"I'm sorry to hear that. Did Mr. Hatton have anything to do with getting you a job in Boston?"

"No," she said forcefully. "As I told you, it was my handiwork that was noticed and commented on. I had a convent education and aside from religion, they emphasized needlework. Many wealthy women bought the garments we created. I never knew it would give me a living."

Brendan looked at Marigold, who had kept a placid face during the conversation.

"And do you speak French?" he asked her.

"Yes, of course. A little German, too."

They looked at one another for a few moments and there was something about her face or mannerisms that struck a chord with him. Was it an actress in a film? Perhaps an advertisement in a magazine whom she resembled.

"Do you have any other questions?" Mrs. Gisriel asked, looking at her wristwatch.

Brendan looked at her earnest face and stopped short of asking anything more at that moment.

"As I told you, he helped me in New York, and we made our acquaintance again here in Boston. That is all. He is married with children," she said.

"And he was seeking a divorce, from what I understand."

"That has nothing to do with me. Our conversations were very general in nature. He never spoke of anything like that. I am sorry that he died. Now, we have to go," she said and stood up, Mari following. As they left, Mari turned around and looked at Brendan, who had that same fleeting feeling of having seen her before.

## Chapter 12

While Brendan was talking to the Gisriel women, Amanda was back in the North End keeping an appointment with Eddie, Saul Somers' friend or protégé, she wasn't sure. She had purchased the lock picks, and it was a good thing they weren't very expensive because she had come to think it was a ridiculous expenditure. They rattled around in her purse as she walked, and she had the distinct feeling that she would never get to use them. A meeting with Eddie would be the only chance, and she was stubborn and proud enough not to give up just yet. If she practiced and got remotely proficient—fine. If not, it wasn't too much time wasted.

Saul buzzed her into the store with a broad smile on his face. "There she is! And she didn't bring her muscle with her!" He laughed at his joke.

"Hello, Mr. Somers."

"Saul! Come on, aren't we on a first-name basis?"

She hoped not, but shortly learned why he had said that. No sooner had she approached his cage than a tall, slim man emerged from the shadows of the shop, his slicked-back hair catching the light.

"Eddie," he said by way of introduction.

Amanda was about to hold out her hand for a handshake but his remained in his pockets.

"Saul here tells me you want to learn the trade."

Amanda looked puzzled.

"Breaking and entering."

"No, no, not at all. I've been working as an investigator for a law firm, and I thought that being able to get into locked desks or rooms might be an asset."

Eddie had a thin, dark mustache and he stroked it. "For what?"

"In case someone is hiding information." As soon as she said it, she felt ridiculous.

"Okay," he said slowly. He reached behind him and pulled a small lock off a table. "Here you go."

Amanda looked at it and him and then Saul. "What am I supposed to do?"

"Unlock it, of course."

"I don't have a bobby pin in my hair," she joked to cover her embarrassment.

"Nobody has ever successfully picked a lock with a bobby pin."

"They seem to in the movies," she said, taking the lock from his hands.

"That's the movies."

She put down her purse, took off her gloves but kept her coat on as the store was cold, except for the heater in Saul's cage. She squinted at the lock and, taking the set of picks from her purse, chose one with a small hook, inserted it into the plug and wiggled it back and forth.

"Doesn't work."

"Of course not." He leaned in further and she got a whiff of the Brylcreem that made his hair shine, even in the dim light.

"Here are the components of a lock. This is the plug or the keyway," he said, indicating where a key would go. "And what you can't see is inside. The cut part of the key," and here he held a key up, "aligns with the pins at the shear line and pushes the driver pins." He continued talking and Amanda couldn't follow the logic at all. "Bingo, it's unlocked," he concluded. "That's the science. *Capisce*?"

"Yes, I'm sure it makes sense, but it doesn't tell me how all these instruments open the lock if you don't have a key."

"That's where the art comes in. You don't just take one of the picks, jam it in the lock, waggle it around willy-nilly and it opens."

Amanda looked at him in consternation. It had been her hope that these tools would do the job that a bobby pin could not, simply by their strange shape. He continued to name all the tools she had in her set, and she realized that this was so detailed and precise an occupation, there was no point in learning it.

She stopped him. "Eddie, I now understand that this it entirely beyond my ability to understand accomplish." He looked disappointed. "It's not that you're not explaining it properly, it's that I don't have the time to practice and perfect what is evidently quite a specialized skill. How about this: I'll give you my set as payment for your lesson. And if I need a lock picked, I'll give you a call. Is that all right?"

Eddie looked at her and then at Saul and shrugged. "Deal," he said, shaking her hand at last.

BRENDAN WAS EXPERIENCING his own frustration in trying to pry information out of Joe Epperson, a master at evasion. The former chauffeur lived in a boarding house, and the landlady was immediately wary of a man in plain clothes claiming to be the police. Even after showing his badge, he had to take out a separate document that he always carried with him for just such doubting citizens. By the time the exchange was over, she seemed to have forgotten who he was asking about.

"Joe Epperson. I know he lives here."

"Why? What's he done?"

"It's police business. If you'd like to be taken to the station and charged with obstruction, I'd be happy to oblige."

She glared at him, turned and stomped up the stairs, turning at the landing. "Well, you coming up or not?" She preceded him up another flight and knocked on one of the doors. "Hey, Joe. Someone here to see you." She turned and went back down.

Brendan waited a few moments and knocked again. "Police. Open up." He heard movement inside and the door was opened by an unshaven man wearing an undershirt and pants who looked as if he had just gotten out of bed.

"What do you want?"

"We can talk here in the hallway, in your room or down at the station."

Joe swung the door fully open to let Brendan in. The room was small, containing only a single bed, a chair and an end table. Joe sat down on the bed, reached for the cigarettes on the end table and lit up. He inhaled deeply and blew the stream of smoke out in Brendan's direction.

"I understand you used to work for the Hattons," Brendan said as he sat down in the chair.

"Yeah."

"How long did you work there?"

"A couple of years."

"Two years?"

"About that."

"When did they let you go?"

"Just last week."

"Did they say why?"

"Sure. They said they had money troubles."

"Really? Just like that?"

"Nah. Hatton said they needed to economize."

"Did you believe him?"

Joe shrugged. "What does it matter? He gave me the sack."

"I imagine you were mad about that."

Joe looked Brendan in the eye for the first time. "What do you think? No warning, just popped it on me."

"Mad enough to do something about it?"

Joe did not respond.

"And gave you a week's wages?" Brendan asked.

"Yeah. But I still have to look for another job."

"Doing what?"

"Whatever I can find."

"Where were you on Tuesday afternoon?"

"Me and Sally went to the movies. It was her half day."

"When you worked for the Hattons, where did you spend most of your day?"

"In the car or waiting for Hatton to come out of some building to be taken somewhere else."

"Did you stay in the garage all day when you were back at their house? It's not heated."

"I would sometimes wait in the kitchen."

"Is that how you met Sally?"

"What's she got to do with it?"

"Did you go into other rooms of the house?"

"No."

"Is there a john in the garage?"

"Sure. Wouldn't want me traipsing around upstairs." Joe stubbed out his cigarette in a small glass ashtray on the end table.

Brendan was writing in his notebook, then looked up. "Do you own a gun?"

"What? Me, no."

"Not a handgun or a hunting rifle?"

"What do you take me for?"

"Do you know how to shoot?"

"Never tried."

Brendan doubted the answer but didn't challenge him openly. He got up. "I don't have any more questions just now, but I may have some as we move along." He was going to thank the man for his time, but the intense scowl directed at him changed his mind.

Brendan returned to the station, disappointed in his day's work, and had Dominic come into his office for a recap of the day.

"How did yours go?" Dominic asked as he got settled into a chair facing the desk.

Brendan growled. "Two very hostile people. Sally and Joe."

"If they're an item, then it would seem they are well suited."

"Did you get to talk to that neighbor?"

"Daugherty? Yes. He's got an interesting set-up. He owns a big house not too far from the Hatton place but lives in this little cottage tucked in at the back with this beautiful dog."

Brendan looked confused.

"Maybe it was the housekeeper's place—I don't know—but he rents the big house to four men. I figure he was the last member of the family and low on funds or something, and that's a good solution to a monthly shortfall."

"These trust fund kids have been having a hard time since the Crash," Brendan said.

Dominic chuckled. "Boo-hoo. It's just him and his dog. He didn't tell me anything we didn't already know except that he didn't see or hear anything on his dog walk that evening. Finding Hatton dead, he hightailed it back to his place and called it in. Then came back in person after he had situated his dog. Didn't want to upset the animal, I guess."

"The coroner called and said only one bullet had struck Hatton. Probably from a rifle, not a revolver. And we've got a missing gun from the Hatton place with a lot of people who had access to where it was stored."

"For some reason, I can't imagine the widow doing it. She's kind of tiny and frail looking."

"Don't be fooled. Annie Oakley was not even five feet tall."

"How do you know that?"

"Reading. Try it sometime. Look, we've got a butler who was fired, and we've got to follow up with him. A chauffeur, likewise let go. His disgruntled girlfriend. A wife who was getting ready to divorce him. A son who may have wanted to hasten the arrival of his inheritance, the daughter—who knows. And who else?"

"I have a feeling there are a lot more 'who elses' out there," Dominic said.

"With her father's permission, Amanda shared some of the research that the firm's former investigator had carried out. It includes Mr. Hatton's visit to two different women on a regular basis."

"Busy guy."

"And someone who lent or gave him a tidy sum that came in and went out of his bank account quickly. Where did it go? And if it's gone, the lender has a grudge, too."

They sat mulling over the evidence to date, knowing there were many more people to talk to.

"Oh, and the bachelor neighbor, Daugherty, confirmed that there are guns in the attic of the big house. I suggested he might want to check that they are still there."

"Why don't you follow up with the quartet that rents the big house and see if they heard or saw anything?"

"He portrayed them as young professional men, suggesting that they were at work all day, but who knows. I'll get to it tomorrow."

## Chapter 13

Her head still spinning from the failed foray into the intricacies of the underworld, Amanda made her way back to the law offices, appreciating the bright lighting and what she considered the straightforward nature of the business. However, the more she thought about Hugh Van Eaton and his interactions with Mrs. Hatton, the more she realized how convoluted the situation was.

"Mr. Burnside?" she inquired, putting her head through the open door of his office since his secretary was not at her desk outside.

"Amanda—Miss Burnside, how can I be of assistance?

She looked at the papers on his desk and for the first time in her life wondered what he did every day. Read documents? Write other documents? She closed the door behind her.

"What sort of case are you working on?" she asked.

He chuckled. "The exciting world of contract law is my specialty. People decide to do something with somebody else and then one party or the other decides not to abide by the original contract. Feeling ill-used or out of a sum of money, they hire an attorney to pinpoint what went wrong and have the other party make amends. If the parties cannot come to an agreement, a judge makes the final determination."

"I've never given it any thought. I always imagined that a jury did that."

"Most of the time, everyone wants to avoid that or going to court. If the case requires only a judge, it means that one person is the decision maker. Some clients shy away from that, others like the odds, if you will. A jury trial is more expensive and time-consuming, of course, and each side must appeal to the members of the jury effectively to win the case."

"When you said more expensive, what did you mean?"

"We get paid by the hour and one of the considerations in any dispute is how much time goes into initial discovery and preparation. It's not just my time, but the time of the staff involved, such as my secretary's time, that of the law clerks and even Mr. Gilbert's time when he was here. You can see how it can accumulate rapidly, and a client who is obstinate despite the evidence can rack up quite a bill."

"How is the bill determined?" Amanda asked.

"We record how much time we work on any given case. That includes all the staff's time. Telephone calls, in-person meetings and so forth. Everyone has an hourly billing rate."

Amanda thought before making her next request. "Do you think I could see Mr. Van

Eaton's billings for the Hatton case for the last few months?"

Mr. Burnside pulled his head back in surprise. "And what does this have to do with your work as investigator?"

"I'm not sure how to put it, but based on what I have observed so far, I get the impression that his visits with Mrs. Hatton—especially the ones to her home—were not entirely related to the impending divorce."

He cocked his head in anticipation of further information.

"If he wanted to see her for personal reasons, then he shouldn't be billing her for professional consultations. As one of the partners, I would think you'd want to know that."

"Does this have anything to do with the death of Mr. Hatton?"

"I don't know just yet. But looking at those billing records might shed light on other things."

DOMINIC HAD FINISHED a heavy lunch and was sitting at his desk, listing the names of the people who still needed to be interviewed for the murder of Eugene Hatton. It was growing exponentially, and he thought he might need to ask one of the other detectives to assist, not only because of the number of people but because the morning paper had taken the opportunity to shine a light on the crime as evidence of the Mayor's failings. If the Mayor was responsible for escalating crime in Boston, the Police Chief would catch the worst of the guff. In turn, the detectives, the beat cops and everyone else in the force would suffer. He thought the murder of a rich man in his own home might make headlines, but it was the least of the city's problems and certainly not due to the lack of police enforcement.

His dozy thoughts were interrupted by a call from the front desk about a man who had been the victim of a robbery. Dominic got up to attend to the citizen and was surprised to see it was Mr. Daugherty.

"Hello," he said facing the distraught man.

"I've been robbed!" he exclaimed.

"Where?"

"At my home!"

"At gunpoint? What did they take? Come back to my desk and you can fill me in. Are you injured?" All Dominic could think was there was a rash of violence in Beacon Hill.

"No, no. You don't understand. Things are missing from the big house. Someone broke into the attic and so much is missing."

Dominic sat the man, who looked as if he were about to cry, down quickly.

"I think you were the victim of a burglary. A robbery is more an in-person event."

"Call it what you will, but those 'professional men' made off with very valuable things."

"Are you saying your tenants took things?"

"Yes! You had asked about guns in the house and even though it was my father who was the hunter, I knew they were stored in the attic. I wanted to check that one of those was not the weapon that killed Mr. Hatton. And I certainly didn't want anyone to think that I had killed him."

"Why would you have? You said you hardly knew him."

"I knew him in boarding school, but we hadn't much contact since. I only saw him on those few occasions that I walked my dog in the alley, and he was very condescending when he saw me. I'm sure he looked down on me because he could still afford his big house and I had to rent mine out to make ends meet. But your question about my tenants had me wondering if I had properly secured the attic and, when the men went off to work this morning, I took my key and went in the house." He had to stop himself, closed his eyes and shook his head.

"Yes, they had been in the attic. They decided that everything there was theirs for the taking. A valuable watercolor and antique furniture had been brought down and placed in one of the bedrooms. Carpets, vases, who knows what else? Once I had looked in the bedrooms and seen that they had availed themselves of whatever they found, I bounded up the hall and saw a key in the lock. Going into the attic, I saw that so many things had either been moved or taken away including my father's hunting rifles." He sobbed at this point and Dominic was at a loss as to how to respond.

"Did you give them a key to the attic?

"No! They must have rummaged through some drawers and found it."

"May I get you a glass of water?"

"Yes," Mr. Daugherty responded softly.

By the time Dominic came back with the water, the man had composed himself and was raking his hand through his reddish gray hair.

"I want to file charges against those men. All four of them. I rue the day that I rented the house to them. They came with excellent references and were fellow brothers of mine."

Dominic was baffled. "Your brothers?"

"Fraternity brothers. Different years, of course. I didn't expect that they would conduct themselves in such a disgraceful way."

"You gave me their names earlier. I assume they are still at work?" Dominic looked at his watch. "Do they usually get home a bit after five o'clock? If so, I can be there with you to confront them about the issue. Strictly speaking, if your lease agreement with them didn't specify that they couldn't rearrange the furniture, or availing themselves of what was in the attic, it really is a civil matter." Just as Mr. Daugherty was about to protest, Dominic held up his finger to silence him.

"But you must carefully inventory what has been moved versus what has been removed. That will make all the difference."

Mr. Daugherty pursed his lips in frustration. "I thought you could help me."

"I believe I am, by being present when you talk to them. I don't have to be there, you know."

"All right," the man said, standing. "Why don't you come to my place, and we can go over together. If I go by myself, I might lose my temper."

As he walked out, one of the other detectives looked over at Dominic and raised his eyebrows and chin to silently ask what was going on. Dominic closed his eyes and shook his head. He hated babysitting.

Brendan came onto the floor and signaled for Dominic to come into his office.

"Who was that?" he asked.

"Daugherty. The guy who called in the Hatton murder. A problem with his tenants and it seems guns at his house are missing, too.'

Brendan exhaled loudly. "How many hunting rifles are floating around out there? It's not like they're the weapon of choice for gangsters."

Dominic tipped his chair onto its back legs. "Perhaps gangsters are more high-class these days," he said, lifting a pinky finger and batting his eyes.

"The coroner finished the autopsy and, based on the information that the doctor had given him, Mr. Hatton had been dead a very short time when the body was brought into the morgue."

Dominic's chair came back down into its more normal position with a slam. "What? Then it could have been Mrs. Hatton or one of the kids. Or a disgruntled former servant. Or who knows who else?"

"We need to find out what showing of the movies Sally and Joe attended and where the family members were during the day. And who this investor in Mr. Hatton's business is and where he was."

"We could always say the butler did it," Dominic said.

AMANDA PRESENTED herself to the bookkeeper and asked for billing records for Van Eaton and two other new attorneys, masking her real intention. "Making sure they're doing it correctly," she said, not meeting any resistance from the woman. The two months' worth of billings she requested consisted of six separate file folders, and she began to peruse them as she left.

The firm had pre-printed sheets where the employee wrote in the date and their name. Beneath were columns for dates and duration of whatever activity had occurred. She could see that telephone calls, research, document preparation and meetings were all meticulously written down by each attorney.

Amanda looked at the two other lawyers' billing notes to get a sense of what a usual span of time for each function was, also realizing that their legal specialties might require different amounts of time. She imagined the phone calls would be the shortest, the research and document preparation the longest and the client meetings somewhere in between. Without knowing what the other two lawyers did, the documentation seemed to follow her original assumption.

Van Eaton had listed Hatton many times as well as other surnames for additional cases in his portfolio but did not indicate if the meetings were in his office or at her home. But what struck her was that, instead of the meetings being an hour long, they were two to three hours long. It wasn't conclusive, but she would bet those encounters weren't in the offices. It could indicate a long lunch or a house visit, both unusual considering it was not, on the face of it, a complex case. As far as she knew, there was only the Beacon Hill house, investments and bank accounts. But even if there was more to the estate, would it really require hours of discussions? Based on Doris's reaction to Van Eaton, she suspected that if he and Mrs. Hatton weren't having an affair of their own, he was certainly buttering her up. At the very least, he was inflating the length of their meetings to increase his billable hours. Or he might have other intentions for Mrs. Hatton once she became divorced. At the worst, he might hasten that situation with the demise of Mr. Hatton.

DOMINIC TOOK his time getting to Mr. Daugherty's house, not relishing what was sure to be a charged atmosphere. The drapes were pulled aside and a face with glasses and reddish hair looked out to see who had driven up. They exchanged pleasantries and made their way to the front of the big house. Instead of ringing the doorbell or knocking, Daugherty used his key and opened the door to the vestibule and then entered the sitting room through an additional door, which prevented the cold drafts from coming into the living area.

They were met with the surprised looks of two young men, each holding a martini glass, as they sat next to a roaring fire.

"Oh, Mr. Daugherty. I see you have used your own key to come in. I would have thought you would ring the bell," one of the men said, not bothering to get up.

"Ralph, there is something I need to talk to you about," the landlord said.

"Care for a drink? Who is your friend here?"

"Detective Barone, Boston Police," Dominic said of himself.

They both stiffened and Ralph got up. "What seems to be the matter?"

"You are the matter!" Daugherty said, pointing at them both.

"Whatever do you mean?" the other one asked.

Dominic tried to interject some calm into the situation, but the landlord was off and running with his accusations.

"You have moved furniture and artwork without permission!"

"I'm so sorry. I didn't realize you would mind."

The seated tenant said, "If I'm not mistaken, it is not usual for a landlord to invade the privacy of tenants without prior notice and permission."

"Whoa, whoa," Dominic said attempting to defuse the quickly escalating situation. "Let's all sit down and discuss this sensibly.

Daugherty was having none of it and did not sit down. "I demand to know who gave you permission to get into the locked attic and take things out. Those are my family's possessions, not some warehouse of items for you to distribute among yourselves."

The noise of the tumult brought another man in his shirt-sleeves from the second floor to the top of the staircase to silently observe. At the same time, yet another man entered the sitting room from the vestibule and stopped short.

"Well, I see we're all here. Let's get down to brass tacks," Daugherty said, finally sitting down on a couch and, with a distasteful look, removing an ashtray and placing it on a nearby table.

"I must say, even with employing a maid and a cleaner, the house looks terrible."

The men exchanged looks.

Dominic tried to gain control of the situation. "There has been a murder not too far from this house. A man shot with a rifle. Your landlord here has informed us that the gun collection in the attic is no longer there. He has every right to know what happened to those guns and, as a police officer, I need to know their whereabouts."

The four men then avoided looking at one another.

Dominic pulled a paper out of his pocket and a notebook. "Which one of you is Daniel?"

The man who had just come down the stairs raised his hand slightly.

Dominic continued with the names of the others that Daugherty had provided just so he could keep straight who everyone was.

"I'd like you to accompany me as I do an inventory," Daugherty said, getting up. Without waiting for Dominic, he strode up the stairs to the second floor, leaving the tenants momentarily astonished before they hastened to catch up.

"Wait, wait!" Robert, the one in shirtsleeves shouted, taking the steps two at a time. Daugherty beat him to the top and, opening the first bedroom door, gasped.

"Good God, man! Are you running a brothel here?"

Dominic and the other men rushed to the open door, and one of them sniggered at the sight of Robert's girlfriend in a garish dressing gown sitting near the window, smoking a cigarette.

"Do you mind?" she said imperiously.

"I certainly do!" Daugherty said. "This is my house!"

She stubbed out the cigarette and looked away.

"And that's my mother's fur stole!" the landlord said, pointing to a dark brown throw at the end of the bed. He snatched it up and slung it over his arm. His face was red and determined as he made his way to a door at the end of the hall. "Here, hold this," he commanded the young man closest to him and putting the fur in his arms. "See, they found a key somewhere," he said.

Dominic noticed it was a simple skeleton key and, even if the tenants hadn't found it, an easy lock to pick.

Daugherty turned on the light and went up the stairs first and said, "See! Just look at this mess!"

The attic was the same width and length of the house itself and it was so full of items that there was only a narrow path from one end to the other. Heavy Victorian furniture draped in sheets took up most of the space; in between the pieces were boxes and cartons, mattresses and box springs, a baby carriage, baskets that looked as if they had been purchased in foreign countries and landscape paintings so huge that sheets didn't cover them adequately.

Dominic had seen many things in his years on the force, but this collection was extraordinary, and he wondered how the owner could know what was there and what was missing.

"See?" Daugherty said, pushing a table aside to expose the empty gun cabinet.

Dominic, a larger man than the owner, tried to move a heavy couch aside to squeeze through the narrow space and hit his foot on something metal. He bent down and looked in the dust to see a hunting rifle. He pulled it carefully out from underneath the couch and held it up.

"Is this one of the guns?"

"Why, yes! That was my uncle's." Both men pushed the couch aside, which was the only way they could both fit in the space and pulled out four guns in all.

"Is this all of them?"

"No, one of them is missing." Daugherty bent down to take a closer look. He turned to see if the tenants had followed them up the stairs and was relieved to see they had not. "Who took them out and why they're on the floor is beyond me," he said, his face red. "And where the other one is…."

"Now, as to them taking things from the attic or moving furniture around, that's up to you to discuss with them and set some ground rules. I would also suggest that you install a more complicated lock on the door."

Daugherty decided to leave the discussion with the tenants to a later date, and he and Dominic left together. As they walked around the back of the big house to his own dwelling, the owner said, "I'm so sick and tired of these entitled people who think they are better than everyone else."

"That may be so, but you could also chalk it up to the inconsideration of the young for old-fashioned things, including the manners with which they were brought up."

"Manners, say you? No, it's all about social class. I know firsthand how cruel people can be when they think you are beneath them. Not handsome enough, not an important enough family, not flashy enough." He quickened his pace, leaving Dominic to go to his car and call it a night.

## Chapter 14

Amanda had learned from Brendan that Marigold had her job at Monsieur Josef's because her mother offered the two of them as a package deal. While Amanda was surprised at her sister's ability to design clothing, she was more impressed by the skill of the women who worked in the atelier, and it prompted her question.

"Would you mind if I observed a bit of their work today?" Amanda asked as she drove her sister to work the next day.

"Really? Whatever for?"

"I'm amazed at how quickly they work, their stiches so tiny and even. I could never do that."

"How well I remember that woman that Mother had come in once a week to show us how to darn, sew a straight seam, mend a hem, crochet a bit and knit. My fingers were small but not dexterous enough to do her instruction justice."

"I remember," Amanda said. "I so wanted to do a wonderful job, but I found it so hard. And here Mother continues with needlepoint, and we are hopeless with a needle."

"Speak for yourself. I've wielded the needle a lot recently and while not of their caliber, I can baste with the best of them."

Amanda laughed. "You make it sound like sword fighting. Isn't basting what you do to a turkey at Thanksgiving?"

She pulled into a vacant spot in front of Monsieur Josef's salon and got out along with her sister. "Introduce me to the women upstairs," she said.

Louisa looked at her in surprise. "All right. I hope I don't confuse their names, although they have their initials on their work smocks."

Louisa put her portfolio in her own small office and they both took off their overcoats and made their way to the third floor and the bright workroom.

"Good morning, Mademoiselle," the ladies chimed as one.

"Good morning, Ladies. I wanted to introduce you to my sister, Amanda. She was so entranced by your work that she insisted on coming up and observing for a bit. I hope that's not an intrusion."

The women looked at each other in surprise that anyone would take an interest but nodded their heads and continued what they were doing.

"May I ask what you are working on?" Amanda asked the first woman, who had bright red hair.

"I am securing the boning in the bodice for this gown," she said, gesturing with her head to the mannequin across from her with a full skirt pinned onto it. "It gives the fabric shape as creating a slimmer waist for the woman who will wear it." She and the others tittered and, looking up, Amanda saw that the mannequin was a short woman with a wide waist.

"What magic you do," she said.

"God made us in all shapes and sizes. But we can fool the eye with the right drape of fabric, color, darts and pleats."

Amanda moved on to the next woman, whom she knew to be Marigold's mother. "That looks very time-consuming," she said as she observed the woman using a long, thin needle and almost invisible thread to sew pearls on a piece of white satin.

"Yes," she answered. "This dress will be a masterpiece when it is done." She had a French accent to Amanda's ears.

"Is it for the Valentine Ball?"

The woman said, "It could never be ready by that time. It's for Miss Valerie's wedding dress."

"Oh, my, that will be lovely. She's an old friend of mine."

"What a coincidence," the woman replied, without expression.

"Where did you learn to do such fine work?" Amanda asked.

The woman stopped for a moment to look up. "I was brought up in Alsace and attended a convent school. That was our form of recreation—sewing." The others laughed. "It didn't hurt that I could also bring in a bit of money with my skill. As soon as the war broke out, I left and came to this country." She stopped speaking at that point and the other women were silent. Amanda sensed there was more to her story, but she wasn't about to share it with someone she just met.

"Well, it's beautiful work. I can't wait to see the finished product."

"Which you will when Valerie and Fred tie the knot," Louisa said, tugging at her sister's arm. "Let's give the mesdames their space so you and I can get to our respective jobs. Merci," she called out.

"Why did you pull me out of there?" Amanda asked. "I was just getting the hang of how everything here works."

"You don't need to. Most of Elenora Gisriel's family was lost in the Great War and she came to America as a refugee. I'm guessing she had her daughter out of wedlock because they share the same surname, but of course, I have never pried."

*Well, I'd like to pry*, Amanda thought since she knew that one of the Gisriel women had something to do with Mr. Hatton. Marigold seemed too young to have been having an affair with an older man—not that Amanda had any experience of such things. However, if she had been seeing Mr. Hatton, why would she need to be working? Unless her mother was the object of Mr. Hatton's attention. But wasn't the mother too old to be a courtesan? Again, if she were, why would she be working in the atelier? Amanda had read about older men retaining a relationship with a former lover, but those were famous people like Napoleon and Josephine, not modern-day people.

On the way to Louisa's office, they saw Marigold coming in their direction.

"Hello," she greeted them.

"Hello," said Amanda. "I guess you didn't recognize me yesterday when I honked the horn and waved at you."

"No, I don't remember. When was that?"

"You must have been on your way home. It was on Storrow Drive."

"I wouldn't have been there. I take the bus home to Commonwealth."

Amanda gave an embarrassed laugh. "Oh, dear. It must have been another girl who now thinks either a wolf is after her or there is a crazed woman who tooted her car horn randomly."

"Well, it wouldn't have been the first time that has happened to a girl in Boston."

"Don't I know it!" Louisa said and they parted with the young woman. "Nicely done, Amanda. But why the interest in Marigold, her mother and where they live?"

"Just filling in some blanks," she responded vaguely.

BRENDAN AND DOMINIC sat at the counter at the diner nearest the station, having coffee and going over the Hatton case to make sense of what they knew so far.

"Joe could have slipped out of the movie, shot Hatton and returned in enough time to exit the theater with Sally. Or maybe he left later when it was getting dark and no one saw him."

"We could always quiz him on the plot of the movie to see if he can remember it all."

Brendan looked sideways at him. "I hope you're joking. Maybe he slept through the matinee. It sounds like a movie that Sally dragged him to, not one of his own choosing."

"Kind of strange, though. You'd think on her afternoon off Sally would have tended to whatever business she couldn't do working every other weekday. Like shopping, getting her hair done, going to the bank, whatever else needs to be done. It would make more sense that they would go to an evening show especially since he was no longer employed. We still need to talk to the ex-butler and find out what gripe he had with Hatton."

"I thought you had done that already."

"No, but we can go together."

"I'm not satisfied with the rest of the Hattons, their whereabouts and motivations," Brendan said, putting his coins down on the counter and getting up.

"Happy families everywhere."

They drove first to the Hattons' home to see if Mrs. Hatton had yet located the former employee's address. She seemed distracted but more composed than the day her husband died. Her daughter, Doris, was home, and she helped hunt through her father's desk for some paperwork while her mother hovered nearby.

"Here it is," Doris said and took out what looked to be a letter requesting a reference.

"I wonder if your husband ever responded," Brendan said, noting that the date of the letter was several weeks earlier. He looked at Mrs. Hatton, whose eyes were wide with confusion.

"I wouldn't know. He took care of the household administration," she said.

"Maybe he sent it from his office. In that case, his secretary would have typed it and had a carbon copy," Doris said.

"Could you give us the secretary's name and the address of the office?"

Doris looked at her mother, who seemed baffled by the request.

"Florence something-or-other," she managed to say. "And his office was downtown."

Doris let out an exasperated sigh. "It's in the Winthrop building."

"That's right, dear. Of course, I'd never been to his office."

"Florence must know of Daddy's passing, but we'll need to retrieve some papers and his personal effects soon."

"We'll need to go in first. There may be some evidence that will help us find out who did this," Brendan said.

The two women looked at one another. "What can you mean?" Doris asked.

"We don't have any motivation for his brutal murder."

The two detectives thanked them for their time and were barely out the door before Doris turned on her mother.

"How could you be so oblivious to what Daddy was doing?"

"What do you mean?"

"Not knowing anything about his business much less where it was. Not knowing that we're in dire financial straits."

"What makes you think that?"

Doris collapsed into an armchair and held her head with her hands. "You let the butler go, you let the chauffeur go, doesn't that tell you that he couldn't pay the bills?"

"I thought we were economizing like the rest of the country."

Doris closed her eyes. "How could you not see that he had something on his mind? It was all about money. I just hope we're not left holding the bag."

"Doris, I wish you wouldn't use slang so much. I never know what you mean."

"It means we could be stuck with the consequences."

Those consequences chose the early afternoon to aggressively ring the doorbell of the Hattons' residence.

Sally had to leave her light dusting of the dining room to answer the insistent noise, muttering to herself, "Keep your hat on."

She opened the door to a large man with a scowling face and regretted having done so as he looked as close to a gangster as she had ever seen in real life.

"Where's Mrs. Hatton?"

"May I ask who is calling?" Sally said in her sweetest tones although the hand that held the door open was ready to slam it shut.

"Mr. Iverson," he said, his feet planted apart as if ready to pounce. "It's about a business matter with Mr. Hatton."

"I'm afraid Mr. Hatton passed away."

"I know that. I want to talk to Mrs. Hatton."

Sally decided that if he meant harm, it wasn't going to be to her.

"Come in," she said and ushered him into the sitting room, holding out her hand to take his hat and coat. He sat, shook his head at her, placed his hat on a side table but kept his overcoat on.

Sally quickly tracked down Mrs. Hatton in her husband's study, puzzling over documents with Doris.

"Somebody here to see you, Ma'am. A Mr. Iverson." She left the room quickly.

Mrs. Hatton looked at her daughter. "Do you know a Mr. Iverson?"

Doris shrugged her shoulders. "Perhaps someone come to pay their respects."

Mrs. Hatton sighed in exasperation at being interrupted in trying to figure out what all the documents in her husband's desk meant and put a sad smile on her face as she went into the sitting room. The man stood up and she was taken aback by the sheer size of him as well as the fury in his demeanor.

"Your husband took ten thousand dollars from me that he was going to invest. He's gone now, and I want it back."

"Oh," Mrs. Hatton clutched her throat imagining that the man might throttle it and backed up a few paces. "I don't know anything about his business dealings."

"That won't wash with me," he said.

Doris had heard the man's loud voice and entered the room. "Can we help you?"

"Yes, you can. I want my money back. Hatton accepted it from me to invest and I don't think he ever did it."

"We are just starting to go through my father's affairs. As you can imagine, his death was sudden. It might take some time to sort through everything."

Mrs. Hatton stood with her eyes wide and said nothing.

"Mr. Iverson, give me your address and telephone number and as soon as we figure this out, we will call you."

"I'll be calling the police instead," he said, jabbing a finger in Mrs. Hatton's direction. "I believe your husband tried to fleece me. You may find the money, maybe not. But I'll get back what is owed me. It could even mean this house," he said, looking around at the high ceilings, the decorative cornices and the expensive furniture. "I'll let myself out. For now."

## Chapter 15

True to his word, Mr. Iverson marched into the police station and demanded to talk to a detective. He got one of the newer men who began to take notes, but once he heard the name Hatton, he knew this was connected to a high-profile case that his boss was working on and went to find him. Dominic saw him going to Halloran's office and interrupted.

"What's up?"

"Someone here about the Hatton case."

"Come to confess?"

"Probably not. He says that Hatton hoodwinked him."

"I'll talk to him," Dominic said, rising from his desk in the corner of the detectives' bullpen and approaching the large man.

"I'm Detective Barone and I'll take your complaint. Just come this way." He picked up a pad of paper and directed the man to an interview room. The man did not remove his hat or coat despite Dominic's suggesting he do so.

"Here's the deal. Hatton took my ten thousand to invest in this building project and now that he's dead, I want my money back."

"For that amount of money, I assume you have a contract."

"Of course I do. What do you take me for? I don't have it on me, naturally."

"This really isn't a police matter. If you have a contract and you think he or his estate owes you the money, you may need to hire a lawyer to sort it out."

The man pounded his fist on the table. "I don't want to pay some shylock to get back what's mine!"

"As far as we're concerned, no crime has been committed. Unless you can prove that."

"You're useless," Iverson said and stormed out of the room.

That was a first for Dominic; usually the berating was lengthier and more colorful. But he had been correct; what did the man think the police could do? And that was a lot of money to invest in some vague building project. Then he remembered that Amanda had been looking into Hatton's finances in preparation for a possible divorce. Maybe she knew what Iverson had been talking about.

Returning to his desk, he called the law firm where she had an office.

"This is Detective Barone," he said.

"Awfully formal, aren't we?" she responded.

"I thought I might have to be since I had to go through a receptionist and then a secretary to get to speak to you."

Amanda giggled. "It does impress people, I must say. Are you looking for Brendan?"

"No, I wanted to ask you some questions that I hope you can answer. Did Mr. Hatton receive a large amount of money sometime in the last month?"

"Yes, he did. About two weeks ago. Very large. Ten thousand. And another amount just last week."

Dominic whistled.

"Why do you ask?"

"Some guy barged in here, claiming that he gave Hatton the money for some project and since Hatton is gone, he wants it back."

"Why did he go to the police?"

"That's what I asked him, and he was very annoyed. I guess he thought we could just muscle our way into the Hattons' house and get it back."

"That would be impossible. Because the money was gone the next day."

"What? In cash?"

"Hold on." There was a shuffling of papers before Amanda came back to the receiver. "It was a money order."

"I don't suppose you have a record of who the payee was?"

"No. He could have left it blank. I know from experience that when you buy a money order, the bank more than strongly suggests you specify a payee. I tried to get a blank one once because I wasn't sure of the spelling of the name, and the teller gave me quite a lecture about how anyone could get hold of it, write in their own name and cash it."

"That was wise advice," Dominic said.

"Yes, except it was only for five dollars, so I thought his reaction was a bit over the top."

"So, what we've learned is that money came into Hatton's account and exited shortly thereafter to an unnamed party. Interesting."

"I'll say." Amanda's mind was whirling while she pondered who would want to kill Hatton. The recipient of the money to hide their tracks? A family member furious that, after all their economizing, a significant sum disappeared?

Dominic was also thinking of the implications. Had Iverson already confronted Hatton only to learn the money was already gone? Did he kill him in anger and only later realize he could get his money back from the estate if he produced a contract?

"You there?" Dominic asked.

"Just thinking," Amanda said. "Things are getting very curious."

"I'll say."

∼

BRENDAN WAS off in search of the butler who finally had a name. Ben Hodges. Did the family call him Ben? Or

Hodges? He shook his head at the pretensions of some of the Boston Brahmin who acted as if they were still in Merry Olde England. And these poor employees who had to wear ridiculous uniforms, actually costumes, for work—an evening coat for the men and black dresses, apron and headache band for the women—were not paid very well despite appearances. Perhaps it was the prestige of the position that kept people in that line of work although he knew in the current economic times any job was a blessing.

As he drove, Brendan thought he might pop into the movie theater where Sally said she and Joe watched a movie. Not to see it, of course, as it was one of those drawing room comedies that you might see on a stage but were now available to all in the local cinema. He could appreciate the dialogue and humor, but all those women swanning around in satin dresses and furs in the middle of day was ridiculous. *They should make more comedies about everyday people*, he thought. *But then we couldn't laugh at them as much because their troubles hit closer to home.*

It was still too early for the matinee, but there was someone in the booth and he showed his badge to indicate that he was not interested in a ticket but needed to talk to the manager. The young man exited the booth and unlocked the door to the theater and pointed to a door at the end of the lobby to the left. The carpet was plush red, and the air smelled of popcorn and cigarette smoke. He opened the door and walked up past the balcony level toward the projection room. Off to the side was a small office where a man was leafing through a girlie magazine.

Brendan knocked on the open door. "Sorry to bother you," he began.

The man practically jumped out of his seat. "Jeez. Nobody comes up here." He smiled nervously and shoved the magazine under other papers on the desk.

Brendan showed his badge and the man paled instantly.

"I just wanted to ask a few questions about how you operate here."

The man stood up abruptly and there was already a sheen of sweat on the man's upper lip, which led Brendan to wonder if this was one of those theaters that did private screenings for particular customers. He let it go but kept it in the back of his mind for some other time.

Brendan remained standing. "When people buy a ticket, can they leave the theater and return as long as they produce it?"

"Sure."

"Is the person in the ticket booth the same one who worked on Tuesday?"

"I'll have to check," he said, turning to his desk and pulling out a work schedule.

"Hank. Yes, he worked on that day."

"Nobody's in trouble, I'm just checking up on something."

"Sure, sure," the man said, greatly relieved. "You know where to find him." He continued to stand, shielding the papers and magazine on the desk, until Brendan nodded and went back down the stairs.

"Hank?" he asked, knocking on the side of the glass booth.

"Yes?"

"You were working on Tuesday?"

"Yes. Matinee until midnight."

"Long day."

"I'll say."

"During the matinee, did anyone leave and then ask to come back in?"

"Just one guy. He looked like he was bored and came back some time later. He probably went to the tavern down the street."

"Why do you say that?"

"Because he looked happier than when he left and smelled like he'd had a snoot full when he got back."

"You sure about that?"

"Look, I don't ask people where they've been and how long. I just take the tickets. I'm just telling you that he's not the first guy to come in with a girlfriend and get bored by a movie. Most guys like the gangster movies, not ones with a lot of folks jabbering in phony accents. He went off to the right and I know there's a tavern a few doors down. That's all I can tell you."

Brendan called in at the address given to him by Doris, a respectable neighborhood where a widow could rent out rooms to people with respectable jobs. The landlady answered the door and told him that Mr. Hodges had moved out a few weeks prior, then helpfully gave him the forwarding address.

He was off to a less prosperous part of town, closer to the docks. Although not as spruced up as the prior home, this, too, was a boarding house, with a postage-stamp scruffy lawn encased by ankle-high wire wickets. Brendan wondered what the point of those was as he could see that neighborhood dogs were able to step over and do their business. The porch steps creaked as he approached the front door, and he was met by an older woman in overcoat, gloves and galoshes who was exiting. She glared at him in annoyance.

"I'm not interested in whatever you're selling," she said.

"I'm looking for Ben Hodges. I understand he lives here."

"Who wants to know?"

Brendan opened the lapel of his overcoat to show his badge and her mouth twisted to the side in irritation.

"What's he done?"

"Nothing as far as I know. He might have some information for me."

"He's not in," she said, turning to lock the door.

"Do you know where he is?"

"Check the Anchor Grill. Down the street and to the left. It's on the corner." She brushed past him, and he caught a whiff of moth balls.

Brendan walked down an empty street of similar two-family homes, children still at school, adults at work and the cold wind keeping all but the hardy from venturing out. The tavern's building was sided with roofing shingles, making it look like it had fallen over, and the two small windows meant the inside would be dark. He opened the outer door, stamped his feet to get the sidewalk slush off and the circulation back before opening the door to the interior. At least it was warm inside, he thought although it looked like just about every other neighborhood tavern he had been in. Nothing like the Oasis, which billed itself as a club, with a doorman, music and well-dressed customers.

There were only two people in the place, the bartender and a tall, thin man, looking down into his beer.

"Ben Hodges?" Brendan asked.

The man looked up. He had a handsome face with a mournful expression. "Who wants to know?"

Brendan was surprised to hear a British accent as he opened his overcoat to flash his badge. He could feel the bartender's eyes on him although he didn't speak.

"I wanted to talk to you about Eugene Hatton."

"I read he died," Hodges said. "It was in the paper."

"Worse. He was murdered."

"You want something?" the bartender asked and at first Brendan thought he was trying to protect his customer before realizing that he was asking about a drink. "Sure, a beer would be good." He pushed his hat back on his head and sat down on the stool next to Hodges.

"The family said they let you go a while back."

"Said it was money troubles," Hodges said. "It didn't look like they were hurting."

"You never know," Brendan said, and the other man nodded his head in resignation.

"You working now?"

"I'm on the graveyard shift down at the factory." He didn't specify which one.

"Those are rough hours."

"What are you going to do?" he replied.

The bartender delivered Brendan a glass of beer and moved toward the other end of the bar so the two men could talk.

"Hatton seems to have been shot with a hunting rifle. What do you know about that?"

Hodges took a sip of beer and turned to Brendan. "I took a rifle from the house, but I didn't shoot anyone."

Brendan tried to hide his surprise at the admission. "Why?"

"Because he had everything, and I was angry. I took one gun—I knew where the key to the closet was. I hocked it in case I needed the money."

"Do you have a ticket for it?"

"Somewhere. I didn't intend to redeem it. What am I going to do with a gun?"

Brendan paused. "Uh, shoot someone?"

That got a smile out of the other man. "Come to think of it, I probably don't have the ticket. I got rid of a lot when I moved from the old place to here. I like to travel light."

"Two questions: do you know how to shoot? And do you think you could find that ticket?"

"I was in the Great War, so yes, I know how to shoot. But I don't think I ever hit any Jerries. And no, I don't think I could find the ticket."

"Do you remember where you hocked it?"

"Somewhere in the North End."

"You were done with your shift at the factory in the morning on Tuesday."

Hodges looked at Brendan. "So?"

"Hatton was shot during the day in the late afternoon."

"It was a rank thing he did letting me go. But I didn't dislike the man. At least, not enough to kill him. I was sleeping in the later afternoon. He looked up over the bar at the clock. "I've got to be going. I should have been in bed already."

He put a scarf around his neck and a snap brim hat on, nodded and left.

Brendan took a sip of beer that had already gone flat and asked the bartender what he owed him.

"Four beers," he replied before telling the cost and Brendan had to chuckle before paying the bill.

## Chapter 16

Brendan and Dominic went to the address provided by Doris to see what sort of business her late husband was involved in and who his colleagues and employees were. The building housed the usual contingent of attorneys, accountants and Hatton Enterprises, which didn't tell them any more than they already knew about what he did for a living. They tried the door, expecting it to be open and, finding it locked, knocked. There was no answer and they wondered whom they could ask about gaining entry.

Just as they turned to go to the elevator, the door opened and a small woman with dark hair looked out at them. For a moment Brendan was stunned by how beautiful she was, with delicate features and large green eyes.

"Are you one of Mr. Hatton's employees?" he finally managed to say.

She looked at him and Dominic and replied, "Who are you?"

"Police," he said, showing his badge.

"What do you want?"

"We'd like to come in."

"You can't look for anything without a search warrant," she said, still blocking entry.

"We'd just like to talk."

She eyed them and reluctantly fully opened the door. The room was bright from the two windows fully illuminating the chaos of papers strewn over the two desks, chairs and floor.

The two detectives stared.

"Did someone ransack the place?" Dominic asked.

She gave a short laugh. "This is my doing. I'm looking for something."

"Sorry, who did you say you were?"

"Florence Dodge. I worked for Mr. Hatton."

"Are there any other employees we should be talking to?" Brendan asked, taking in the shabby furniture and the worn linoleum floor.

"I'm his secretary. Was. Also, the only employee."

The notion that the late Mr. Hatton was the head of any enterprises, much less a booming business, evaporated.

"What were you looking for exactly?"

She looked from one man to the other. "Some paperwork."

"That's obvious," Dominic said.

They waited for her to clarify.

"I was owed some money and I'm looking for the paperwork to prove it. I imagine I'm going to have to sue the estate for back salary."

"I should think you'll want to tidy up this mess or you won't find anything."

In a flash she was right in front of Brendan's chest her index finger extended. "You're not going to be telling me what to do here. This is a mess of his own making and I have no intention of cleaning it up, whether I find the document or not."

Brendan carefully moved her hand to the side. "There are other people looking for documents and money, too. I suggest you hand over the key and we'll lock up for you."

"Not on your life. Eugene paid me well—until he didn't a few weeks ago. I'm owed that money." Her eyes welled up. "He was getting a divorce from his wife. We were going to get married."

"Had he hired an attorney?"

"Sure." She turned to the larger of the two desks and opened the top drawer and pulled out a business card and handed it to him. It was Mr. Burnside's firm.

Brendan showed it to Dominic, who looked puzzled, but another look from Brendan telegraphed that he would explain later.

"Are you going to the funeral?" Brendan asked, handing back the card.

"Looks like I won't be showing my face. I don't even know if his wife knew what was going on."

The two detectives shrugged their innocence.

"There's a Mr. Iverson who says he had a contract with Mr. Hatton. As his secretary, I'm sure you prepared that document."

"Iverson? No, I don't recognize the name. I haven't come across any such contract."

"That's all right, the man assured us that he had a legitimate copy. It's really not our business."

"What are you going to do now?" Dominic asked.

She pushed the papers off one of the chairs, sat down and started to cry. "I'll figure something out. Why don't you go now."

"Sure thing," Brendan said and preceded Dominic out the door.

"Tough stuff," Dominic observed as the elevator doors shut on them.

"Even worse. Hatton couldn't possibly have hired someone from Burnside's firm to represent him. That would be a conflict of interest since Mrs. Hatton already had Van Eaton representing her. The firms make sure to check on these things so there is no embarrassment, either."

Dominic shook his head. "So, he just made it up for her sake. Hatton sounds like a real piece of work."

"Let's go talk to the son and daughter again and see if they can remember anything else that will be of use."

Without calling ahead, the two detectives went to the Hatton residence, assuming that so soon after their father's death, surely the two would be at home. When they arrived, Sally the Surly, as Dominic had begun referring to her, answered the door, barely disguising her enmity.

"Who shall I say is calling?" she asked.

Brendan kept a straight face and said, "Chief Inspector Halloran."

"And Detective Barone," Dominic added.

"Step this way," she said and ushered them into the sitting room. "Is it Mrs. Hatton you're wanting to see?"

"No. Is Christopher available?"

"I'll see," she said, sauntering off.

They sat down and removed their hats.

"I almost said Gary Cooper when she asked who we were. Alas, I don't look much like him."

"Grow a mustache and next time say you're Clark Gable."

They waited and looked around the opulent room. Silk upholstered loveseats and chairs, a huge Persian carpet in muted colors and a few shelves with small statues of shepherdesses. They looked at one another and Brendan observed, "Maybe one of the enterprises was wool."

"Or sheepherding," Dominic said.

"Or fleecing people."

A few minutes later, they heard footsteps on the heavily carpeted stairs and stood to greet Kit Hatton.

"Hello, gentlemen," he said in his most condescending manner. He took a cigarette out of a gold case without offering one to them and lit it with a lighter on the round table in front of them. "You wanted to see me?"

"Why don't we sit down?" Brendan suggested since their host hadn't done so.

"We had some new information and wanted to know your whereabouts in the early afternoon Tuesday."

"I thought we had already been through that," he drawled.

"Refresh my memory, if you don't mind."

Dominic took out his notebook while Brendan maintained eye contact with the young man.

"As I told you before, I woke late, had breakfast, pottered around and then had a late lunch with friends. And then a drink at my club." His tone was wounded as if anyone should suspect him. He took a drag of his cigarette and blew the smoke out of his nose. "Did you return at any time?"

"No, you can ask…right, it was the staff's half day. But no, I was out and about most of the day."

"*Most* of the day?"

"All of the day until this time."

"I meant to ask you before, when you said you had a late lunch, what time was that exactly?"

"I'm not sure. I bumped into some friends from boarding school, and we found a place to eat. Perhaps about one-thirty?"

"Where did you eat?"

"I was ambling along Milk Street when I saw my friends. It was so cold and windy that we took shelter in the nearest thing to a restaurant that we could find. I couldn't possibly tell you the name."

"I'm sure you can if you try," Brendan said with a smile.

"It wasn't really a restaurant. It was a tavern. With a name like 'Bob's' or something. We all got a drink to warm up and asked if they had any food aside from the dreadful pickled eggs in a jar over the bar that had probably been embalmed there for ten years." He chuckled at his wry observation and tapped the ash from his cigarette in a marble ashtray. "So, we asked the bartender if we could order food in from nearby. He acted as if nobody had ever made such a request."

Dominic gave a side glance to Brendan but held off from making a comment about what it might look like for some toffs going into a tavern and 'ordering out.'

"As it turned out, there was a steak place around the corner and rather than facing the elements, we sent him— or someone who worked behind the scenes there—to put in an order. As you might imagine, it took some time, and we had a few more drinks before the excellent T-bone steaks and pommes frites arrived."

"And how long did the lunch last?"

"I couldn't say."

"Try."

"A few hours. We were all a bit tipsy and could see the wind had not abated, so we stayed put as long as we dared. We drew lots and my friend Howard was stuck with the bill. Good thing as I had very little cash on me. Then we went to the club and had another drink."

"Did your father supply you with an allowance?"

"Why, yes," Kit responded, surprised at the question.

"Why were you here last week? I would think that classes would be in session."

"It's Intercession. A break at the end of semester, which for some reason ends in mid-January. Silly calendar, really. Some people go skiing, the lucky ones go to Florida or the Caribbean, others stay in the dormitories and the unfortunate ones go home."

"I would think the unfortunate ones are those who had to stay back in the dorms," Brendan said.

Kit shrugged and blew out a stream of smoke. "It was not great fun here I can tell you. My parents barely speaking, my sister trying to jolly everyone along." He shivered.

"Will you be graduating this spring?"

"I hope so. That is, if my father has already paid my tuition. He hasn't always been timely in that department."

"Are you aware of any money difficulties in the family?" Brendan asked.

Kit was slow to answer. "My father alluded to that from time to time, but I always suspected this was his way of trying to stem my spending."

"That's not a bad thing, is it?"

"It is when all your friends seem to have no reins on their allowances." He stopped short, realizing that his comment sounded like whining. "But I understand. Business has been difficult."

"What business was your father in exactly?"

Kit opened his eyes wide and gave a short laugh. "Now that you mention it, he was never very specific about what he did."

"Was he expecting you to join the family business after you graduated?"

"I hope not. We never had that conversation. I made it clear to everyone that I wanted to go to New York and try my hand at acting."

Dominic looked down at his notebook and refrained from saying what was going on in his mind.

"Were you aware that your father withdrew a large sum of money recently?"

"No. He wouldn't have confided in me anyway." He paused. "How much was it?"

"Twelve thousand dollars."

Kit didn't seem particularly surprised by the large sum.

Brendan asked, "Do you know anyone who would want to harm your father?"

"Heavens, no. He was just a regular Boston businessman. Who would want to kill him?"

"We hope to find out. Thank you for your time."

Kit stubbed out his cigarette and rose to leave.

"One more thing, did you ever go hunting with your father?"

"Yes, it was a thing when I was younger. All four of us went although my mother was not too enthusiastic. My father thought all gentlemen ought to learn to shoot. For those occasions when you might be invited for a weekend."

"How nice. By the way, could you tell me if your sister is at home?"

"Why, yes. I'll get her." He gave an unctuous smile and walked back up the stairs.

Dominic exhaled loudly. "This is heavy lifting."

They made additional notes while waiting for Doris to appear a few minutes later. They stood at her approach.

"Hello, Officers. I hope you are getting closer to finding out who did this."

"Please sit down, we just needed to ask a few more questions."

Doris sat and leaned forward as if intent on what they were going to ask. She was not a pretty girl but what they used to call handsome: strong, even features and warm brown eyes.

"Can you give us more detail about how you spent the day Tuesday?"

"As I've told you, I had lunch with the girls who came out with me. We went to Valerie's father's club. It's a monthly thing. The conversation was a lot of chit-chat about who was seeing whom and so forth."

"What else did you talk about?"

"If you think those girls have any interest in politics, world affairs or the state of humanity, you must be thinking of another group. We chat and then meet again the next month to resume the latest antics, travels, dating and engagements of our fellow debs."

Brendan thought it unusual that both Amanda and Doris seemed to have the same opinion of the group but persisted in meeting with them monthly.

"To be honest, I would have loved to go to college and be with women with more interest in the world, but it was not to be."

"Why was that?"

"Not from lack of interest. Lack of funding. My father decided he would rather throw away his money on my brother's vague ambitions and prospects than on someone who hoped to make a difference." She stopped short, realizing she might have said too much.

"That must have been hard."

"It was and it still stings. But now that I am dating Kit's roommate with all intentions of being engaged and married within the year, I suppose I have then fulfilled my parents' aspirations of maintaining our standing in the social order."

Brendan flipped through his notes from their first interview. "After lunch you went…."

"To the Museum of Fine Arts. I felt I had to cleanse myself from the silly chatter of lunch."

"Who is your favorite painter?" Brendan asked.

"What? Well, I admire Sargent very much."

That was an interesting choice, Brendan thought, since she had exactly the strong features that were depicted in his portraits of society women.

"Yes, they are wonderful. You stayed until what time?"

"It was getting dark, and I wanted to get a taxi home."

"You don't have your own car?"

"No. That privilege is reserved for Kit," she said with a small smile.

"How is your mother holding up?" he asked.

"She's an emotional woman in the best of times and this has eliminated the reins on her hysteria."

"She has just lost her husband of many years, after all. It is the most difficult of losses."

"I apologize. I didn't mean to sound heartless. But every time there is an outburst, she seems to need Mr. Van Eaton to come and calm her down. He was already here this morning. If you don't mind me saying so, I think his attentions have gone beyond representing my mother in some of her family's issues. I don't even know what they are since she won't tell me. And when I ask, she bursts into tears again."

"It will be difficult for you all for a long while," Brendan said and thanked her for her time.

"I'll get Sally to show you out," she said, which the two men insisted they did not need, not only because they knew their way out but facing the gorgon was not appealing.

The sun was trying hard to appear behind the clouds, but the cold wind had them turn up their collars against the gusts.

"So, everyone in the family knows how to handle a gun. And a gun is missing. That doesn't narrow things down at all."

"Do you think Mrs. Hatton could do that?"

"Her dramatic reactions could be manufactured, for all we know. And maybe just a way to get Van Eaton to show up more regularly."

"The young pup didn't seem surprised about the money being withdrawn. Do you think he swiped it?" Dominic asked.

"It seems anything is entirely possible with that family."

## Chapter 17

"Let's pop over to the North End," Brendan said to Dominic, who was at the wheel.

"Good thinking. I could do with a hot coffee and something to tide me over until supper."

"That wasn't what was first on my mind, but I'll take your suggestion."

Dominic sighed as they were hit with the smell of warm bread, pastries and coffee that his favorite bakery offered.

The owner's high school daughter was behind the counter, her parents having gotten up before dawn to light the ovens and prepare the dough. Afternoons were slow, with a slight pickup in customers getting a loaf of bread before dinner. She looked up from her textbook and gave them a smile.

"Hello, Officers."

"Two espressos and two sfogliatelle."

She turned to the elaborate machine that hissed as she began the process of preparing the coffee. Tongs were used to take out the powdered sugared pastries and put them on two plates. They sat down at a small table and Dominic took his first bite.

"Heaven."

"Since you're between girlfriends, you could wait another year for her to come of age. Just think of the benefits of marrying into a baker's family," Brendan said.

"It would be wonderful except I would be twice the size in no time."

When the espresso was ready, she brought it over to them on a tray along with small glasses of water.

"*Grazie*," Dominic said. "If it weren't for this miserable weather, I would say I'm in heaven."

"When we're done here, we'll make a visit to Purgatory."

Dominic's brows met above his eyes. "What do you have in mind?"

"Relax. I want to stop at Saul's place and see if that might be the place Hodges hocked his gun. Not that it's the only place in Boston or the North End. It's a needle in a haystack, but as long as we're here."

After they had finished their snack, Brendan assured Dominic that the pawn shop would be the last stop for the day. It was already getting dark when they drove the four blocks to Saul's place, dim yet still open if you pressed the button outside. Saul looked up from whatever he was reading in his wire cage and buzzed them in.

"Good evening, gentlemen. What have you brought me tonight?"

"Hey, Saul. As usual, all we've brought are questions."

"Go ahead. The night is young."

"You have any guns?"

Saul laughed, showing a gap between his front teeth. "You've got to be joking. Of course. But all of them are legit. No serial number filed off or anything."

"I wouldn't expect less."

Saul moved to unlock himself from the cage and Brendan added. "I'm not looking for a handgun but a hunting rifle."

Saul turned and said, "Sure. We had one. Bought it and sold it a week ago or so."

"DO you remember who brought it in?"

"Sure. Tall, skinny, sad-looking guy. A limey."

"You sure?"

"Yeah. I asked him where he was from, and he hesitated before saying London. As if he just got off the boat and walked in here. His accent wasn't so strong, so I guessed he might have lived in the States for some time. Looked down on his luck."

"Did you really think it was his?"

"Hey, we don't ask for ownership papers, do we? As far as I know, it belonged to his dear old dad. Unless proven otherwise."

"It very well could be proven."

Saul shrugged his shoulders. It was part of the business.

"Do you remember who bought it?"

"I don't. Let me look at the receipt book to see when it sold exactly. I don't remember the same guy redeeming it. Hey, Eddie" he called.

The man stepped out of the shadows and nodded his head in greeting.

Saul flipped through the pages of his book. "You remember who got the hunting rifle? It looks like a day I wasn't here."

Saul showed them the book.

"Yeah, I was here that day," Eddie said. He ran his long fingers down the row of sales and redemptions. His dark brows came together as he thought. "I was a bit preoccupied that day with family things," he said. "But I remember he was well dressed and didn't say much. It was as if he didn't want to admit he had come in looking for a gun. The transaction was quick, and he paid in a stack of tens."

"Old, young? Color of hair? Anything else about how he looked?" Brendan asked.

"Maybe late twenties, no, early thirties. He didn't take off his hat and he always had his head turned away."

Dominic shook his head. "Tall, short? Thin, heavy?"

"Just your average medium kind of person."

"Gee, that helps."

"What can I say?" Eddie said. "He obviously didn't want anyone to know he was in here."

"Did he have an English accent?"

"No. Posh, although he was trying to hide it."

"Thanks, Eddie," Brendan said. "At least we know it was a guy."

"Maybe he bought it for somebody else," Dominic added.

"It could have been a woman in disguise," Eddie remarked.

"Why do you say that?"

"Kept gloves on the entire time. Kept turning his head away so I couldn't see the face. Small feet. And a whiff of hand cream."

"Great. That helps a lot."

When they were out onto the sidewalk, Dominic said, "Since when is Eddie an expert on hand cream?"

"I heard he was quite a ladies' man."

"Him? I guess it depends on what you're looking for in a man."

They reached the car.

"Can't wait for the heat to kick in," Dominic said.

"We don't have much to go on in this case. Broken promises from Hatton, plenty of resentment from his children, two missing guns and a lot of money that came and went pretty quickly. They always say to follow the money, but where the heck is it?"

"Maybe Mrs. Hatton got her hands on it and is not letting on," Dominic said.

"Could be. Unless all that behavior is an act. Or one of the kids. Kit didn't seem all that surprised about a significant sum slipping through the family's fingers."

"How hard would it be for him to forge his father's signature?"

"You'd think the bank would be leery about that large of a transaction."

"It didn't sound like the secretary had got her hands on it. Unless she did and she's not saying. But then why would she be ransacking the office? She'd have left town by now if she had her hands on it. What about this other woman he was seeing?" Dominic wondered.

"I haven't figured out if it was the mother or the daughter, but they both were tight-lipped about what was going on. And if they had just received that sum of money, why are they still working?"

"If it were me and ten grand fell into my lap, I'd be long gone," Dominic said.

"Where to, exactly?"

"Someplace warm."

They got to the station just as the heater had started to thaw their cold feet. No sooner had they got inside than Brendan was alerted that a Mr. Van Eaton was waiting for him in one of the interview rooms.

Without taking off his coat or hat, Brendan went into the room, shook hands with the man and said, "Let's not meet in here. Unless you were going to make a confession." He added a smile, but Van Eaton was not amused as he followed him back to Brendan's office.

"What can I do for you?" he asked.

Van Eaton was a handsome man but very staid in his demeanor. Full of himself, some would say.

"I wanted to inform you that Mrs. Hatton intends to take out a restraining order."

Brendan waited for the other shoe to drop.

"Against Mr. Iverson. He has persisted in calling her and threatening her to reclaim some funding that he insists was provided to the late Mr. Hatton."

"I understand it was a large sum and he has already been here to get us to assist him. Obviously, we cannot unless it was physically taken from him. And you know that it's the court that will grant a restraining order, not the police."

"You don't need to tell me my business. I wanted you to know that we are taking action against the man. Based on his prior behavior, I fully expect that he will ignore the order, in which case I'm here to make you aware that a call could come from the Hatton residence at any time. I would like you to respond in due haste when that happens."

"And you don't need to tell me my business. That is what we usually do."

The two men looked at each other in silence.

Brendan added, "I know that Mrs. Hatton has lost two of her male servants recently. Does she feel unsafe in her home?"

"The other servants do not live in. You've noticed the house is large and her son is often not at home. I've suggested additional locks on the outer doors and that she might want to hire a bodyguard."

That was new to Brendan; he had never heard of anyone who was not a major public figure having a bodyguard.

"As her advisor, that might be best," Brendan said. He didn't say what he was thinking, which was it was over the top and perhaps just another way to fatten the lawyer's fee.

"I checked in at Mr. Hatton's bank about the deposit and withdrawal. I thought it unusual that such a large sum would be withdrawn without some hesitation on the part of the bank president. As it turned out, he said Mr. Hatton was in the habit of depositing and withdrawing large sums. So, the fact that he presented himself at the bank to do such a transaction didn't raise any eyebrows."

"Too bad."

"Indeed. Well, that's all." Van Eaton got up, then added, "Have you made any progress on finding out who killed Mr. Hatton?"

"We're working on it. Early days."

"Hm," the attorney said and shook Brendan's hand unenthusiastically before leaving.

Brendan made sure to look down at Van Eaton's feet. They were on the small side, but he had to take Eddie's word for it. What was small for a man?

A short time later, Dominic put his head around the open door. "I don't know if you heard, but the bullet is typical for a Winchester."

"That gets us nowhere. Both Hatton's and Daugherty's missing guns were Winchesters."

"Agreed."

"Don't you think it odd that someone walked into the alley carrying a rifle and nobody noticed anything?" Brendan asked.

"Like who?"

"A gardener—although in winter they're not around much. A maid looking out the window or a resident doing the same. Someone didn't walk several blocks to get behind the Hatton house with a rifle tucked under their arm unnoticed. Unless the rifle was already stashed nearby. Or it came from a nearby house."

"Such as the Hattons' own house. Or Daugherty's," Dominic said.

"That's seems easy enough. But then there is the disposal of the gun. Where did it go? If it came from the Hattons' house, it could still be there. If it came from Daugherty's, it might have been chucked into the nearby vegetation. I think we need some officers to comb the area at the back of the house and the rest of the alley."

"That'll be some job."

"It has to be done."

## Chapter 18

Amanda called Louisa at work that afternoon and told her sister that she had a highly confidential request.

"What is it?" Louisa asked, on her guard.

"I need to know about Marigold."

"What? What for?"

"Didn't I just say confidential?"

"By that, I thought you meant you wanted me to do something on the sly, not that you wanted me not to know what for."

"I wanted to know where she has previously lived, her birthdate, anything about her. Can't you just get into some casual conversation, share something about yourself and ask her about her life?"

"That's all well and good except she's not in today," Louisa said.

"What?"

"She called in sick and won't be in until tomorrow."

"That's interesting," Amanda said, noting that it was shortly after with the death of Mr. Hatton.

"It is?"

"Doesn't Monsieur Josef have records for his employees? Addresses? Vital statistics?"

"What are you on about? I don't have access to that. Jeanne is the one who does that sort of stuff."

"Well, find out from her! Tell her you wanted to send a get-well card because she has been out sick."

"That's very unlike me," Louisa insisted.

"I know that, but Jeanne probably doesn't. Can you do that?"

Louisa gave an exaggerated sigh and said she would.

A few minutes later, Louisa appeared in Jeanne's office. "Is Mari in today? I haven't seen her."

"She wasn't feeling well. Her mother, as well."

"Oh, dear, I hope it is not some bug going around. It's best they stay at home, then."

"I agree," Jeanne said.

Louisa started to leave and then turned around. "You know, she's such a sweet girl. Always helpful and in a good mood. I think I'd like to send her a get-well card. I've got an idea," she said with animation. "I'll get a card and we'll all sign it!"

"That would be lovely," Jeanne said.

"Oh—I don't have her address."

"Here, I'll look." Jeanne opened a file drawer to her left and took out a folder. It was only for a moment that she leaned over with a paper and pen in hand to write down the address, noting the birthdate on the inside of the flap of the folder.

"Thank you, Jeanne."

It was minutes later that Louisa was back on the telephone with her sister.

"Got it!"

"Good job, Watson."

"Wait—isn't he the slightly dense sidekick to Sherlock Holmes?"

"I never thought so," Amanda fibbed. "What do you have? That's great. Now I'm off to the library."

"What for?"

"To see if I can track down her family."

"But you already know her mother," Louisa persisted.

"But we don't know who her father is or was."

"You will pick me up after work, won't you?"

"Of course. But you need to get a get-well card first and make sure everyone signs it. Got to go now!"

Amanda put on her coat, grabbed a note pad and drove her car out of the business district, past Boston Common to the main branch of the library. She was fairly certain that birth records were likely not stored at the library, nor could she get them from whichever governmental agency held them. But she had another ace up her sleeve.

There were only a little more than two hours left that the library would be open, so she had to act fast. She went to the reference desk and asked to see back issues of the several New York City newspapers for a particular time span. She knew that hospitals published births and she had a feeling she would discover Marigold's paternity. But as she flipped through the pages, she saw that the listings typically only had a surname and the gender of the child. There was Gisriel, girl, in the ***Brooklyn Eagle,*** but she was no closer to finding out who her father might be.

An hour later, Amanda showed up at Louisa's workplace, ready to take her home.

"A bit early, isn't it?" Louisa asked.

"I'd like to beat the traffic." In a whisper she asked, "Do you have the card?" Then she said in her normal voice, "Good. We're going to deliver it in person."

Louisa looked at her sister. "Why all the mystery?"

"Because it *is* a mystery. We'd better stop and get some flowers; don't want to show up empty-handed."

The roads were congested with commuter traffic, buses and trams, but they made their way up Commonwealth Avenue and managed to find a parking spot.

"This feels really strange, Amanda," Louisa said.

"It's fine. You take the lead in being sympathetic while I keep my eyes peeled."

They found the name Gisriel on the bank of nameplates inside the vestibule on the fourth floor.

"They don't even need to buzz us in. I wouldn't like living in a place with no doorman and little security," Louisa said.

"Don't worry, I'm sure you never will. I don't know what I dread more, climbing four flights or taking this rickety elevator," Amanda said as they pulled back the metal grate, stepped inside, pushed it back into position and pressed the floor number. It creaked into action and moved slowly upward.

Louisa got the giggles. "I'll bet there is some poor man in the basement hoisting us up. I hope he doesn't let go."

"When I was on my tour in Vienna, one of the buildings had what they called a paternoster—an open elevator that was in constant rotation. You had to time it perfectly to get in and jump out at the floor you wanted."

"Are you making that up? That's horrible. I'm sure I would be standing there forever trying to get the courage up to get in and then paralyzed with fear about getting out."

"We only observed other people using it. The tour guide didn't dare have us try it."

As the elevator jolted to a halt, they both became quiet and exited onto a silent floor.

Amanda was about to press the bell on the side of the door when Louisa stopped her hand.

"Maybe we should have called before coming," she said.

"Element of surprise." She pushed the button and heard the ding-dong chime on the other side of the door. They waited and thought they heard movement.

"Suppose they don't let us in?" Louisa whispered.

"If they ask who it is, you speak."

Louisa shot her sister a stern look but before she could say another word, the door opened a crack and Mrs. Gisriel's eyes could be seen.

"Is that Louisa? Is something wrong?" she asked as she opened the door further.

She was dressed in street clothes, not the gray work uniform from the salon, and the color in the peach sweater made her look years younger.

"No, we were concerned because we heard you were under the weather."

"Well, yes and no. It's Mari. She gets migraine headaches and needs me to be with her."

"How nice. Our mother always pampered us when we were ill. Everyone at work assumed something was more serious like influenza," Louisa said.

"Oh, no, nothing like that. Somebody at the salon must have misunderstood."

They were still standing in the living room and Louisa introduced her sister to Mrs. Gisriel. They shook hands.

"Yes, I remember you came into the workshop."

There was an awkward pause that Louisa quickly filled by holding out the card to the woman.

"Everyone at work was worried. If she's not too ill, may we see her just for a moment?" Louisa asked, giving her the flowers so both the woman's hands were occupied.

"Of course, she is just through here." Mrs. Gisriel motioned toward a short hall that led to two small bedrooms. "I'll just put these in water."

Louisa knocked on the open door and said, "Mari—how are you?"

The young woman looked pale, and her hair mussed from lying in bed, but was otherwise glad to have company.

"How kind of you to check in on me," she said, sitting up more erectly and smoothing the bedspread.

"Wires got crossed and someone at work thought you were in dire circumstances," Louisa said with a laugh.

"Oh, no. Perhaps my mother exaggerated."

"I'm sure not. I've brought you a get-well card."

While the conversation was taking place, Amanda was surveying the room and hoping to get a better look at the framed photos on the top of the dresser. She gestured to the window to the side of the bed.

"What a great view you have of the garden. And that tree! I'll bet it's gorgeous when it comes into leaf in the spring."

At the mention of the tree, Marigold turned her head to the fading light, and she sighed. Amanda looked over to the photos and saw one of Marigold in a white dress as for her graduation, one a younger image of her mother and one of a handsome man who was instantly recognizable to Amanda.

"Is it a chestnut tree or an elm?" Amanda asked. "It's hard to tell when there are no leaves on it."

"An elm. I love looking out on it." She turned back to the sisters. "Can you stay for tea?"

"Oh no," they both hastened to say. "Just checking to make sure you're all right."

"Thank you. That is so kind." Marigold made as if to get out of bed.

"We'll see ourselves out. Our parents will be wondering why we're late getting home."

They passed Mrs. Gisriel who was exiting the kitchen with the flowers in a vase and who looked surprised that they were making for the front door.

"Won't you stay for tea?"

"Thank you, but we must be going. Here's to a speedy recovery," Louisa said.

They didn't speak as they went to the elevator and pressed the button. They could hear it make its way up to the fourth floor. The doors opened and they pulled back the grate. Once back outside the building, Louisa asked her sister, "What was so important that we had to make an in-person visit? And what was all that business about the tree and the garden, which looked rather shabby, actually?"

"If you lived with lesser means, you would be happy to have any touch of beauty or nature. But it was a way to get closer to look at the photographs on her bureau."

"What did you see?"

"Nothing much in the garden. But the photographs? I believe I saw a young version of Mr. Hatton."

## Chapter 19

Brendan arrived at the Burnside home at six o'clock weary from the day at work, frustrated at not having put much of anything together and hungry as well. Simona answered the door, a smile on her face having known Brendan from his visits to her family's restaurant in the North End.

"Your coat?" she asked.

"I'm not staying long, just picking up Amanda for dinner."

"Still…," she said and insisted on taking his hat and coat.

"Hello," said Mrs. Burnside as he was ushered into the sitting room. She was in her usual place near the fireplace working on some needlepoint. What began as some trepidation on her part as to his relationship with her daughter had changed over time and she found him respectful and interesting.

"Please sit down."

"I won't be long. We'll be dining out," Brendan said as he sat on the sofa next to her.

"Oh, you young people. Always gadding about. You need to spend more time in the family circle. And you know Cook makes the best roasts."

"I can smell it already," he said.

Mr. Burnside, having heard voices, came in from his study and greeted Brendan, who stood up to shake hands.

"Why would the lovebirds want to sit around with us over dinner? They obviously want to be alone."

Brendan's face colored at the term 'lovebirds,' although the term was accurate.

"Daddy, are you tormenting Brendan?" Amanda asked, overhearing part of the conversation as she came down the stairs. She and her fiancé shared a chaste kiss before she sat down in an armchair.

"Sherry, anyone?" Mr. Burnside asked.

"Thank you, yes. Chilled to the bone today in more ways than one," Brendan said.

"What do you mean?" Amanda asked, alarmed.

As he accepted the glass from her father, he said, "I had the strangest sensation that someone I talked to today is someone I've met before."

"A déjà vu experience?" Amanda asked.

"I didn't phrase that quite right. I mean more like a doppelganger."

"What's that?" Mrs. Burnside asked, having only focused on the 'gang' portion of what he had said.

"Someone who looks very much like someone else."

"I suppose there is a finite arrangement of facial features," Mr. Burnside observed as he sat close to the fire. "Seeing as most of us are from Western Europe, it stands to reason that we all look alike."

"How can you say that?" Mrs. Burnside said. "If we all look alike, how could someone fall in love with another person—they might as well fall in love with somebody else."

"Good point, except you are excluding the effects of personality and allure," he smiled.

She chuckled as his comment and continued her work.

"What I meant is that the gradation of our hair color goes from blonde to reddish to dark brown. And shades in between. Have you ever met anyone with green hair? Or blue hair?"

"Mrs. Reynolds," Amanda said. Brendan looked puzzled.

"Oh, really, Amanda," her mother said.

"She's a woman who goes to our church and has very white hair. It appears she uses some kind of bluish rinse to make it appear even brighter. Except sometimes it really looks blue."

"Like the bluing people use for laundry?" Brendan asked.

"I certainly hope she's not using that!" Mrs. Burnside said.

"But back to your experience," Amanda prompted.

"It's not important but it was unsettling. Folks you wouldn't know," he added, fearing for the inquisition if he gave her the name of the young woman. He then changed the subject and asked Mr. Burnside for clarification about a point of criminal law that might apply to one of his cases, again without mentioning the individuals involved.

Amanda was curious about what he was up to, but once the discussion ended and they had finished their drinks, they got up and said goodbye before retrieving their coats.

"Where to?" she asked as they got into his car.

"I thought we might try a German restaurant that I used to frequent."

"That sounds perfect for a cold night," she said. "Do you know the owner?"

"I don't only dine where I know the owner, you know."

"But it doesn't hurt," she said, noting how on those occasions when he did, they got favored treatment.

The windows facing the street were partly obscured by half curtains and the upper portions were hazy with steam from the warmth inside. They stamped the slush off their feet in the vestibule and then entered the cozy establishment that smelled of cooked meat and sauerkraut.

"I think we have to order beer, don't you?" he asked her.

"When in Rome…."

A stout waitress in a Bavarian costume appeared at their table and returned shortly with two foaming steins.

"Oof," Amanda said, seeing how much she was expected to consume.

"Tell me about your day."

"Wait, shouldn't we look at the menu first?"

"I forgot to mention that they don't have one. There is one dish prepared for the evening and it's take it or leave it."

"Do you know what it is?"

"No, that's the fun of it. Now, what did you do today?"

Amanda took a sip of her beer, nodded in appreciation, took a deep breath, and then decided to tell him all about going to the Gisriel home.

"First, don't get mad at me."

Brendan's closed his eyes for a moment. "Let me have it."

"As you know, Louisa works with the Gisriel women, and they had called in sick. So, I thought it might be nice for the girls at the salon to send a get-well card to her."

"Okay…."

"It makes a much better impression if you deliver such a card in person. I agreed to accompany Louisa to deliver it."

Brendan stared at her.

"What?" she asked, her face all innocence.

The waitress's arrival with two steaming plates of food delayed the conversation.

"Either one of those women may be suspects in a murder," Brendan said, his dark brows in a scowl.

"I hardly think they are," she answered. "Doesn't this beef smell wonderful? Tangy."

"It's sauerbraten. Traditionally made with ginger in the gravy. And *Kartoffelkloesse*, those little dumplings."

"And red cabbage. I don't think I've ever had that before."

"As you cleverly avoid the topic," Brendan said.

She tried her best charming smile.

"And don't try to bamboozle me," he said, relaxing his stern look. "Back to the Gisriel women. What do you know?"

"I know they came from Alsace. At least the mother. I saw a record of the daughter being born in New York. And that the mother is an excellent seamstress, evidently much in demand."

"Here's what I know," Brendan said. "That the mother made the acquaintance of Eugene Hatton after the war through some relief agency for refugees."

"Really? How did you find that out? Oh, this gravy is excellent."

"I interviewed them."

"Interesting. Because when Louisa and I went to deliver the card and the flowers, I happened to see a photograph of what appeared to be a younger Mr. Hatton on Marigold's bureau."

"Perhaps he helped them, and they are fond of the man," Brendan said.

Amanda put down her knife and fork. "That's not what I think. I think he's Marigold's father."

"Based on what evidence?"

"All you have to do is look at her eyes and the shape of her face. If you saw the photo, you would see the resemblance."

"I have seen the resemblance. And you may be right. But it wasn't with Mr. Hatton, whom I never saw in a photograph."

"Who then?"

"It's right in front of your face, Amanda."

"You mean you?"

Brendan laughed. "No. Doris Hatton."

She was stunned and took a moment to ponder. "I think you're right." She returned to eating her meal while she thought. "So, what does this mean for our case?"

"*Our case?*"

"We're working together on this, aren't we?"

"I wasn't aware of that."

"Of course we are. A private detective is either at odds with the police, which I think is an unnecessary obstacle, or works with the powers that be."

"Amanda, you're not technically a private detective."

"I know that. But I plan to remedy it."

"How?"

"If I work as an investigator for my father's firm, I may be eligible."

"There are some other requirements," he persisted. Brendan ran his fingers through his hair. "That might upend everything. I don't know of any other female private investigators—not that it makes any difference. But it could jeopardize my job if the Chief thinks I am assisting a private party or passing information to you."

"You haven't so far, have you? Mostly I've given information to you. And we've been able to work harmoniously together so far."

"I'll have to give it a lot of thought," he said.

"Nothing seems to have turned up in this case so far. Has anyone found the murder weapon yet?"

"No. The officers scoured the wooded part of the alleys and came up with nothing. A needle in a haystack."

"I think we have to look deeper for motives rather than try to find physical evidence that could so easily be disposed of."

"It seems the murder weapon was easily acquired, whether through theft or a pawn shop purchase. Saul's shop, to be exact."

Amanda's eyes widened.

"You may think this is all very cerebral, figuring out who did it. But remember, somebody most likely went to the trouble of stealing a gun and killing a man. And we still don't know why. But if they were that determined to do away with him, they might want to do the same to someone who is looking for them."

## Chapter 20

Dominic had the task of going to the bank the next day to look through the bank records of the Hattons—mother, son and daughter. He didn't expect to find a corresponding amount of the missing money for no one would be so obvious as to deposit it in their bank account if they had swiped it. But just to make sure, he leafed through the ledgers, only to find that Kit Hatton seemed to be consistently overdrawn on his account. What surprised him more was that there were no penalty charges, which certainly would not have been the case if a mere mortal was to be overdrawn. Once again, different rules for different folks.

One of the tellers saw him looking through the ledgers, shut down his cage and had a quiet word with the bank's president. A few minutes later, Dominic was asked to come into a back room where the teller was encouraged to talk to the detective.

"I had two unusual requests yesterday," the teller began, looking to his boss for reassurance.

"Don't worry," the president said.

"First, a woman came in who said she was Mr. Hatton's secretary. She showed me a passbook, so I had no reason to doubt that, and I had seen her come in before to conduct some of his business. Then she said the family wanted her to close the account. I thanked her for her concern because I had read that he had died. I also told her that I couldn't close it with instructions from her; it was his family or the estate's attorney who had to come in directly. She looked annoyed and then asked me to update the passbook. It seemed to me she was trying to find out how much was in the account, and I'm not allowed to do that."

"We value the privacy of our depositors," the president said, putting on an even more serious face.

"Then what happened?"

"She pulled the passbook back and muttered something like, 'We'll see about that.'"

"Could you describe her?"

"Small, very attractive, dark hair."

Dominic nodded and made a note in his small book.

"There was another person asking about the Hatton account," the teller said, waiting to be asked to elaborate. Dominic nodded.

"A gentleman who frequents the bank, a Mr. Iverson, came in and asked about the Hatton account as well. He received the same answer: that we couldn't divulge any information and it was in the family's hands."

The president patted the teller on the back.

"How did he take it?"

"He was furious and slammed his hand down on the counter. He demanded to talk to my superior. I made the mistake of telling him that he would get the same answer and he reached in and try to grab me."

"Bad business, that Iverson. Has a temper."

"I lurched back, and he looked around the room as if there were some way to get to me but the swinging door to our stations is locked. The guard heard the ruckus and started to come our way, thank goodness. Mr. Iverson left at that point."

"That's helpful information, thank you."

As Dominic exited, it occurred to him that someone may have redeemed the money order at another bank in Boston. With any luck, that might be true, even though that someone could have cashed it out of state although he personally would never walk around with a money order of that value. He made the rounds and, although it took him some time, he finally found who had received the cash and things seemed to make more sense.

When Dominic returned to the station mid-afternoon, he revealed his findings to Brendan, who took the information quietly.

"Isn't that amazing?" Dominic asked.

"Not really," Brendan answered. "But it eliminates several people as suspects. One thing that would have helped us is using some newer investigative techniques that a cop from Chicago learned from a study he did in Europe."

"Wait a minute. Do you mean that the Chicago Police Department sent one of their own on a fact-finding tour of Europe? Why didn't we think of that?"

"I certainly wish I had. Not only did he tout the hiring of high school graduates for the force, but he talked about more scientific approaches to investigations."

"Such as?"

"Testing for gunpowder residue on the hands of suspects. If we had been able to do that at the Hattons' house, we could have either confirmed or eliminated the family members," Brendan said.

"And Daugherty, too, although I don't think there was any motive for him."

"My guess is the Chief wants to try some of these techniques, and if they make our job easier, why not?"

"What about the high school graduate piece? I'm all in on that but there are many on the force who wouldn't qualify."

"I expect if he endorses that, he'll have to grandfather them in. But just think of the quality of the recruits we would get."

"Smart asses, just like you and me," Dominic answered.

"You forget I have a college degree. So, I'm a smarter smart ass."

"I bow to you," Dominic said with an elaborate gesture.

After a moment, Brendan asked about Daugherty's tenants. "Do they have any plausible motive for doing in Mr. Hatton?"

"Not that I can put together. But we can interview them again. This time in more detail than just about the stolen gun or precious artwork moved around."

They decided to wait until after the young men would most likely be home from work before driving over to the big house. All the lights were on, signaling they might have finished for the day, and the door was answered by one of the young men, the maid presumably gone. He wore a smoking jacket and had what looked like a Manhattan in his left hand and a lit cigarette in the other and appeared to be baffled why Dominic was back and who the other man was.

After a brief introduction, it clicked, and he opened the door wider. "Just in time for cocktails," he said.

"Alas," Brendan said. "We're on duty, as they say."

"Who's going to check?"

"I'm Chief Inspector Halloran, this is Detective Barone, who I think you've met. And you are?"

"Bill Underwood. What's this about?"

"Are your roommates here?"

"Robert and Daniel. Ralph hasn't come home yet."

Since the young man still stood in front of them, Brendan suggested that they come inside where they could talk more comfortably. Bill led them into the sitting room where a backgammon board sat open on a low table next to an ashtray full of spent cigarettes. A fire had been lit but was not throwing off much heat, so the detectives decided, after looking at it but without consulting each other, to keep their overcoats on as they sat on the sofa.

"The Daugherty family evidently never had a chimney sweep in, and the draw on the fire is awful. I wouldn't be surprised is old Mrs. D was stuffed up in the flue." He laughed but stopped abruptly when he saw the look on the detectives' faces. "Sorry. A tasteless joke."

"Do you have any reason to believe that your landlord has committed any unlawful acts?"

"No, no. Not of that kind. Although barging in here and snooping around is not what any of us expected. And making such a fuss about moving the furniture and artwork." Here he made a face indicating what he thought of that, "Well…."

"How did you come to rent this place?"

"We're former fraternity brothers," he said, pointing to a wooden crest above the fireplace with three Greek letters on it. "Daugherty was a member well before our time and from what I heard, it was in the doldrums until a few years before we joined. Nonetheless, when we were looking for a rental, somehow we got connected to the old boy. Did you know they used to call him Rufus because of his red hair? They used to tease him with the 'Rufus Rastus Johnson Brown' song." He laughed. "Somebody did it at one of the reunions and I thought he would have a cow." He laughed again.

"What's going on?" a voice said from the staircase. It was another of the roommates, who identified himself as Robert. "Hello, again," he said, smiling at Dominic. "What's up now? Have we trodden on the threadbare carpets too much?" He plopped himself into an armchair. "What are we drinking?" he asked.

The detectives did not respond to that question.

"We're trying to follow up on the missing gun from the attic. Has anyone else been in the house recently?" Brendan asked.

Both young men laughed. "Don't tell Daugherty, but we've had several parties since renting the place. All very quiet since the old boy lives just around the bend."

"A few people or many? And how many parties would you say?"

"Only a dozen or so," Robert answered.

"And fewer than a dozen people at any given time. We didn't want to make too much of a ruckus."

Brendan sighed. "Co-workers? Old friends?"

The young men looked at one another and shrugged. "Not too many co-workers, mostly frat brothers and college friends."

"Could you put together a list of who you've invited?"

"We could, but you know, you invite someone you know and someone you don't know shows up. All in good fun," Bill said.

"It's not like we have a guest register," Robert said.

"Were the parties down here or did people roam around the house?"

"You're beginning to sound like old Rufus now. Of course, people had access to the rest of the house. The facilities are upstairs," Bill said.

"When I was here, the key to the attic was in the lock," Dominic said. "If that was the usual situation, anyone could have gone into the attic."

"That freezing cold, dusty mausoleum? Why would anyone go up there when we have four perfectly steam-heated bedrooms?" Bill laughed at his observation.

"This is no laughing matter. Mr. Hatton may have been killed by the missing gun. And one of you may be implicated."

That sobered up the two young men quickly enough.

"We don't know anyone who knew Mr. Hatton. Or had a reason to kill him," Bill said.

"Not that you know of," Brendan responded.

## Chapter 21

"What a mess," Brendan said as he drove Dominic back to the station. "Too many loose ends and too many secrets."

"I can't remember, did we ever ask Mrs. Hatton if she was competent with firearms?" Dominic asked. "Kit referred to the 'family shooting parties.' He said all four of them. I wonder how good a shot she was or is."

"Good question. Let's call it a night and make diagrams tomorrow," Brendan said, getting a puzzled look in return from Dominic. "You know, lining up all the players and drawing lines connecting them."

"Is this something you learned in some college math course?"

"No, and even with mapping out all the relationships, we might not come up with any answers."

BRENDAN STOPPED by his apartment and freshened up before heading to the Burnsides' home, where he had been promised a home-cooked meal by Amanda and Louisa since their parents had a social engagement.

Just as he was walking up the steps, Simona was coming out the front door.

"Good evening," she said with a mischievous smile.

Brendan stopped in his tracks. "What's going on?"

"A very elegant dinner is being prepared for you."

"So, the kitchen is in chaos?"

She giggled. "Enjoy your evening," she said and pulled her collar up closer under her chin.

Seeing that she had left the door ajar, he opened the door without ringing the bell, locking it behind him. Things were not in chaos, but he could hear anxious voices floating out from the kitchen into the dining room. He took off his coat and hat, hung them in the hall closet and walked quietly toward the back of the house.

"Amanda, no! You have to be ever so careful with the egg whites. If you even get a speck of egg yolk in the bowl, it won't whip up correctly."

"Who told you that? Does it matter if it's all going to go in the same pan eventually?"

Brendan proceeded carefully and was surprised to see Rob Worley in the dining room nursing a drink and smiling. The man always appeared calm, relaxed and fully in control of things.

"I'm surprised to see you here. Who's minding the store?" he asked about the nightclub.

"They let the boss get some time off occasionally."

Brendan knew that José was the major investor although they liked to pretend it was Rob for some reason. Coming from a rich South American family, José probably didn't want to get his hands dirty with the details of the business—the hiring and firing, doing the books or ordering the staple of the enterprise, the alcohol. He had made a killing during Prohibition, and it looked like the nightclub business was booming.

"Rob, who are you talking to?" Louisa asked, coming through the swinging door to the kitchen. "Oh," she said, seeing it was Brendan.

"You look chic as always," he commented, and she twirled around, showing off the white apron that concealed most of her dress.

"Now what?" Amanda called from the kitchen and Brendan went through to see what they were concocting. "Louisa? Hello, Bren," she said extending her face to be kissed.

"What are you making?" he asked, peering over her shoulder.

"A soufflé," she answered as if it were obvious.

"That's an ambitious dish for a first timer."

"I would hardly call myself a first timer. Novice, perhaps. Louisa has been sneaking around behind my back picking up tips from Cook, who wisely departed the premises before we began. Anyway, one of those women's magazines said that every young man likes a soufflé."

Brendan looked askance. "I think every female editor thinks that's what a man wants when he would rather have a steak, medium-rare. But I can't wait to sample whatever it is you're making."

"What an excellent, diplomatic answer. Louisa just needs to come in and do whatever additional needs to be done. The salad course is ready, and I'm knackered and in need of a drink." She took off her apron and pushed through the door to the dining room. "No wonder Cook is often in a grumpy mood. Cooking is difficult! I don't know how your mother does it with your large family."

"Years of practice."

"And cheerfully, too," Amanda said, taking a glass of whiskey that Rob had poured for her while he handed another to Brendan.

Louisa came out of the kitchen. "Dinner's in the oven. We just need to wait for the timer to go off. Hey—wait for me!" Rob poured her a glass of whiskey as well.

"Cheers." They held up their glasses and took a sip.

"Here's to the chef—or chefs." Rob raised his glass again.

"You'd better wait to see how it turns out before you celebrate," Amanda said.

"Oh, ye of little faith," Louisa added.

"I'll just set the table while we're waiting." Amanda moved to the large breakfront and took linen placemats out of one of the drawers. "How was your day?" she asked Brendan.

"Confusing and I feel we're no closer to figuring out what's going on except now we know who got the money."

Amanda looked up from what she was doing. "And?"

"All will be revealed," he answered. She handed him the placemats and went to get plates and utensils.

As he put them out on one end of the long table, he continued, "When I went to college, the idea was that I would be educated and able to get a good job when I was done. And then do that job diligently and save for my future. These young men—"

"What young men?"

"The ones I spoke to today, the renters of the man who discovered Mr. Hatton, seem to have not a care in the world."

"Perhaps they don't," Rob said.

"Well, they're certainly not saving their salaries by renting that huge house and a maid besides, throwing parties and drinking the night away."

"Why did the neighbor rent to them anyway?" Louisa asked.

"I suppose because they had the money to fritter away. And the house may be a valuable asset but he's probably cash poor. And they were fellow fraternity brothers from Brown. Although they hastened to add that the landlord was a member years before when it was not 'the house' to pledge."

Amanda shook her head. "People can be such snobs. That Van Eaton fellow who works with my father also went to Brown. Small world."

"How do you know that?" Brendan asked.

"I've been in his office and saw the diploma on the wall." She paused. "Do you think he knows the renters?"

"Oh, yes," Rob said quietly.

All eyes turned to him.

"Are those 'the lads' from the club?" Louisa asked.

"One and the same," he said. "Each one is running up quite a tab."

"Why do you allow people to do that?" Louisa asked.

Amanda and Brendan exchanged looks but said nothing.

"We'll settle up soon, possibly at a small discount. It keeps them coming in when they know I am so benevolent." Rob smiled and took another sip of whiskey.

The timer dinged in the kitchen and the sisters rushed in to see the final product.

"It looks wonderful," Amanda said.

"The key is we have to serve it immediately before it deflates," Louisa said.

"You take it out—I'll get the salad," Amanda said, feeling a sense of urgency.

It came out to the table swaddled in a towel and placed carefully on a trivet in the middle of the table. The men stared at the majestic height of the soufflé and were urged not to jostle the table, or the meal would be ruined. Obediently, they carefully sat and admired the puffy brown top in the high-sided ceramic dish.

"It's beautiful. Dare we eat it?" Brendan asked.

"Of course. That's the point. Prepare for the deflation," Louisa said putting a spoon into the crusty top. As soon as she broke the surface the full aroma of the cheese escaped and everyone sighed, then laughed at their initial reaction.

After the portions were served, Rob said, "This is magnificent. But I'm afraid I can only have a bit. Got to get back to work." He gave his glowing smile to Louisa, who pouted in disappointment.

"Bravo," Brendan said. "Rob, my good man, you clearly won't starve."

Rob got up less than ten minutes later, apologizing to them all and was escorted to the front door by Louisa.

"I hate to be a wet blanket, but I've got an early morning and a lot of organizing to do," Brendan said to Amanda.

"What's that about?"

"I'm going to get the folks connected to the Hatton case together in the afternoon."

Amanda's eyes lit up.

"And yes, you probably need to be there."

## Chapter 22

The next morning Amanda could scarcely keep her mind on her work, which consisted of reviewing all that she knew after scouring Gilbert's notes on Mr. Hatton's comings and goings before his death. She also went over what information she had taken from the taciturn Hugh Van Eaton on the occasions when she had asked him to elucidate Mrs. Hatton's intentions. The only other tasks she had were trying to make sense of the deposits and withdrawals to the account of a different client who claimed his partner was cheating him. This was the case that she had been informed about early on in her work at her father's firm, at which time she had been told that the partners continued to work with one another. It was a case that nobody wanted to follow up on, and over the past few weeks she came to see why.

The least difficult part of her work was filling out a time-card for the bookkeeper. She kept her eyes on her watch, having set aside an hour for lunch before heading to the police station for the assembly of people associated with

Mr. Hatton. She hoped that Brendan had been successful in getting them all together but didn't dare add to the pressure by calling him to confirm. He had said one-thirty and that's when she intended to show up.

Noon finally arrived and she chose to go to the sandwich shop down the street from the law firm where a man and his wife had carved out a space on the first floor of an office building for their busy breakfast and lunchtime trade. He nodded to her as she came in and took a place in line, observing the other customers. They were mostly office workers who in pleasanter weather might sit outside in the small parks dotted around the downtown area. But at this time, in the blustery weather, they might scurry back to their offices, brown paper bag in hand, and find a quiet spot if their business did not have what was now called a break room to consume their lunch. She exchanged pleasantries with the owner as he rang up her order and then sat in one of the wicker chairs while his wife prepared a sandwich for Amanda. She felt butterflies in her stomach and couldn't understand why. Yes, she had a hand in the case and had given Brendan useful information, but at the same time she worried about the implications of what she had contributed. What if her assumptions of Marigold's parentage were incorrect? Had that put Brendan's career in jeopardy? Had he come to the same conclusion when talking to the Gisriel women? He hadn't said. The more she thought about it, she realized that he had been close-mouthed about what he knew while she had revealed everything she had discovered. A tinge of resentment was overcome with the feelings of anxiety she felt about the afternoon's assembly of family, acquaintances, alleged business partners, a mistress and possibly a daughter. Could Brendan sort it out? Or had he already done so and didn't feel he could share it with her.

Amanda arrived at the station and found a seat at the back of the conference room where only Dominic was present. By tacit agreement, they did not speak to one another or make eye contact, something she would hold to when Brendan came in.

A large man, his hat still on and his overcoat flapping open, burst through the open doorway and, scanning the room, saw Dominic rearranging the chairs around the long table.

"There you are! Have you found the money yet?" he asked.

"We've got some other people coming and we'll explain at that time."

"What's to explain? It's my money." His chin jutted out in a belligerent pose and Amanda felt his eyes on her, but he probably assumed she was the clerical staff and of no interest or help for his situation. He looked at the number of chairs and chose one toward the middle where he could observe everyone.

The Gisricl women came in next, the mother with her eyes downcast and Marigold looking defiant. She nodded slightly to Amanda and wondered if the large man at the back was another police officer. As they hesitated before choosing a place to sit, Mr. Daugherty came in, his red hair standing up from static electricity when he removed his hat. Recognizing her from the day of the shooting, he, too assumed she was a secretary there to take notes.

Minutes passed before Joe and Sally came in together, both looking put out that they had been called in on short notice. Moments passed before Ben Hodges walked in, more subdued than the pair, holding a snap brim cap in his hands, running his fingers along the edge as he cast an eye over the group. Brendan, right on his heels, excused himself and walked around to give Dominic a piece of paper. June, the other maid, came in, looked surprised at the number of people in the room and decided to sit near the other help.

Hatton's secretary entered, her sharp eyes flicking over the assembly of people she did not know before she recognized Iverson and sat toward the front, steering clear of him. Brendan was anxious to begin but the Hattons weren't there yet. He whispered something to Dominic, who left the room and returned a few minutes later with Mrs. Hatton, Kit, Doris and Van Eaton a respectful distance behind.

After the rustling of them sitting, taking in the presence of some familiar and other unfamiliar faces, they focused their attention on Brendan.

Van Eaton was the first one to speak. "I assume you have called us here for a briefing on the demise of the late Mr. Hatton," he said in his most imperious tone.

"In a manner of speaking, yes," Brendan said, still standing at the front of the room. "We all know that it was on Tuesday when Mr. Hatton came home that he was confronted by someone who shot him."

Mrs. Hatton gasped and shut her eyes momentarily.

"For some reason, Mrs. Hatton didn't hear the gunshot, just the barking of a dog, while she was in the house. It was only later, when she wondered why her husband hadn't arrived, that she went down to the garage to see if his car was there. Instead, she was met with a gruesome scene. She managed to go back upstairs and collapsed, not knowing that Mr. Daugherty, one of their neighbors who had been walking his dog, had already come upon the open garage door, seen the body and rushed home to call the police. The operator asked him to go back to the Hattons and wait for our arrival."

Brendan began to slowly walk from one side of the room to the other. "But first, I want to talk about the matter of the missing money."

"Here, here!" Iverson said, pounding his fist on the table.

"What? Do you think he was killed while being robbed?" Van Eaton asked.

Several of the people around the table looked puzzled and then concerned at the mention of missing money, especially the former and current staff of the Hatton family who knew they would be the first people implicated in a theft.

"No, not at all. We located the recipient of the funds, and I can assure you that they were given by Mr. Hatton willingly."

Mr. Iverson burst out, "I went to the bank to find out what happened, and they were of no help whatsoever. And let me tell you, that money was an investment in a real estate deal for which we were partners. He never put it toward the purchase of that building—he put it in his account and gave my money to somebody else!"

"You'll have to take up the issue with the Hatton family on how to retrieve the funds. As far as we're concerned, he had every right to give what was in his account to whomever he wanted."

"Just a minute!" Iverson said, his face growing red with rage.

"I didn't ask for it. He just gave it to me," Mrs. Gisriel said.

All heads turned in her direction, puzzled at who this woman was.

"He gave it to me for Marigold." The room had become quiet, and she continued. "He was her father."

Mrs. Hatton put a handkerchief up to her face as if she would faint and then all eyes were on Marigold.

"You said you had met while he was doing relief work after the war."

She averted her face and murmured, "Yes. It was a brief thing, and we regretted the indiscretion. But he left New York shortly thereafter before I knew I was pregnant."

"I don't believe you," Mrs. Hatton said.

"An investigator working on behalf of Mrs. Hatton uncovered that her husband visited the home of the Gisriels several times. He assumed that he was having an affair with Marigold," Brendan said.

"I don't believe you, either," Doris said, although at that moment the resemblance between her and Marigold was evident. "Why had you hired an investigator, Mother?" Doris asked.

Hesitating, she replied, "Mr. Van Eaton insisted. I was preparing to divorce your father," she said.

Both of her children turned shocked faces in her direction.

"What were you thinking?" Kit asked.

"You don't have to say anything else," Van Eaton said, putting a hand on her arm to prevent her from speaking.

"In case you hadn't noticed, we hadn't had a conversation of note in many years. Our financial situation had become worse."

Noises of scorn came from the people at the table who had been let go as well as Sally and June, still employed.

"As if those economies were going to save you all," June said boldly to the shocked face of Mrs. Hatton, who had never heard a sharp word from the woman before.

"Back to the money," Iverson said.

"Mrs. Gisriel and her daughter didn't know he was in Boston until several months after they relocated from New York. Hesitant at first, it was a relief to reconnect with the man who had been so compassionate to her years earlier. The fact that Marigold found the photo of her young father and kept it in her bedroom speaks volumes about the need to bond with him."

"So, you blackmailed my husband?" Mrs. Hatton asked.

"No, he readily gave me the money. I didn't ask for it. He wanted to make sure that Marigold could pursue her education."

"*My* money, you mean," Iverson said.

"I didn't ask where it came from. He told me he was wealthy," Mrs. Gisriel said.

"*Was* is the operative word," Kit said. "I may not be able to go back to college."

"Florence, his secretary, knew about him depositing the money at the bank. After he died, she went to the bank and tried to retrieve it. Not only did she not have the authority to do so, but it was already gone. Mr. Iverson tried the same thing with the same results. No, the Gisriel women could have had a reason to be angry with Mr. Hatton, but they weren't. And after he gave her mother the money, what possible reason would they have to kill him?"

"Revenge," Mrs. Hatton said.

"There are many in this room who could fit into that category. Mr. Iverson, for example, a hot-headed man, could very easily have lost his temper, come to the house in Beacon Hill just as Mr. Hatton was returning home and confronted him. If he had, Hatton would have been smart enough to say that he would get the money for him the next day when the banks opened. If that were the case, Mr. Iverson would certainly not have wanted to kill him. In fact, he still believed the money was in the account or he wouldn't have gone to the bank to try to get it back."

"Of course, I didn't kill him. But I will get my money!" He glared at Mrs. Hatton.

"And Ms. Dodge, the loyal secretary, was counting on that money as Mr. Hatton had promised her that, once he divorced his wife, they would start a new life together," Brendan said.

"What! That's impossible. You cheap—," Mrs. Hatton said.

"Hardly cheap, Lady. That was going to be our getting-out-of-town stash. I knew he had it from Iverson and I was looking for his passbook so I could present it at the bank as if on behalf of my boss. But no dice."

"Again, I don't think Miss Dodge had a motive for killing Mr. Hatton. Although she may have thought so after he died and stiffed her on the money," Brendan said.

Florence glared at him.

He continued, "And I don't believe she somehow found a rifle and went to his house to kill him. No, the crux of this is the weapon. We scoured the alley behind the house, under the leaves and the ivy and the wooded areas nearby and, of course, found nothing. This murder was planned. It was not an impulse. Someone knew Mr. Hatton's habits, when he would come home from work and could walk up to him and shoot him without Hatton making a move to protect himself. The killer was known to Mr. Hatton. And I'm sorry to say that the remaining people in the room knew him well and had plenty of motives."

## Chapter 23

Brendan paused to take a sip of water but continued to stand.

"Others who can be eliminated are June and Sally, June because she had no particular grudge toward Mr. Hatton, and Sally, because she was watching a matinee showing at the time of the murder."

The two women glanced at each other with a bit of triumph in their expressions.

"However, Sally's boyfriend, Joe, slipped out during the movie, according to the cashier, and came back in sometime later with alcohol on his breath. The man was unclear about how long he was gone and assumed he had gone out for a drink at the tavern up the street. But he could just as easily have got into his car and driven up to Beacon Hill, done the deed and come back."

"What!" Joe cried out.

"There was a gun missing from the cabinet in Mr. Hatton's study. Anyone who worked there—or still works there," Brendan looked over at Sally, "could have got the gun for him. Who knows where the gun is now?"

"Well, I never," Sally sputtered.

"Or perhaps it was Ben, still angry at having been sacked, who did."

The former butler looked injured but didn't respond.

"I think he took the rifle before he was gone from the Hatton residence all right, but it seems he pawned it because he needed the money."

"See," Ben said, feeling exonerated.

"Somebody bought the rifle just days before Mr. Hatton's death and it wasn't someone with an English accent. In fact, whoever bought that gun tried very hard to conceal their face. We don't know if it was a man or a woman."

Van Eaton let out a groan. "So, you really don't know much of anything, do you?"

"To make things more complicated, there was another missing gun. From Mr. Daugherty's house. I should say from the big house that he rents to four young men, fresh out of college and anxious to be on their own. They have parties, girls over and access to an attic with family heirlooms and, as you might guess, hunting rifles, one of which was missing when Dominic went up there with the owner."

"And they also pilfered some of my family's paintings and furniture to decorate their rooms," Daugherty said.

"Which gun killed Mr. Hatton? One of his own? Mr. Daugherty's? Someone else's? We can't know because we can't find the weapon. We have to look for the motive."

Van Eaton looked at his watch conspicuously as if he had better things to do.

"All the Hattons were proficient with a rifle as they used to have shooting weekends. Kit could have been furious that his father had told him that tuition for college was too great an expense under the current circumstance. Doris, who may have suspected that her father was having an affair, could have assumed that part of the family's money was going elsewhere. That combined with her anger that Kit got to go to college and was frittering away his opportunities while she never got the chance is a powerful motive. And both have vague alibis of where they were that afternoon.

Mrs. Hatton grasped the hand of each child who sat on either side of her.

"And what about Mrs. Hatton? She knows how to shoot a rifle. She was home all alone on the staff's afternoon off. Taking a nap. She assumed that the information the investigator had provided proved that her husband was having at least one affair, if not two. And all he talked about was economizing when she suspected the money was leaving the family entirely."

"I say," Van Eaton protested.

"Wouldn't she be better off a widow than having to go through the humiliation and expense of a divorce? All her problems tied up in a bow and the sympathy of the community, to boot."

Mrs. Hatton put her face into her handkerchief as if she were sobbing.

"And was that an act when we got there? The hysteria, the assumption that you had taken tranquilizers and couldn't be coherent enough to answer questions? One gun was missing, but who is to say that was the gun that was used to kill your husband? Perhaps you used another gun and replaced it in the cabinet."

"No, no!" she said.

"And now we come to Mr. Van Eaton, the helpful, ever-present attorney. Yes, he is years younger than she but what is an age difference when he knows that the illusion of failing finances was Hatton's way of stashing his running-away-from-home money?"

Van Eaton glared at Brendan but said nothing.

"And then we come to the day of the murder itself. Mr. Daugherty, a near neighbor, is walking his dog in the alley, sees the murdered man and rushes home to put his dog in a safe place while he calls the police and then returns to the Hatton residence, very agitated, very helpful."

Daugherty nodded his head gently, acknowledging the sentiment.

"And we come to find out that his tenants have ransacked his attic and moved things around, to his great dismay. He even brings Detective Barone up there to discover one of his guns has gone missing and he blames the roommates. What we come to find out is that the roommates are all Brown graduates, from the same fraternity, no less. They do not hesitate to inform us that their 'house' was a prestigious one on campus, not the pokey little group that it was when Mr. Daugherty was there years before. And another interesting fact is that Mr. Van Eaton is also a Brown graduate and a frequent guest in Mr. Daugherty's rental. So, who took which gun that killed Mr. Hatton? The gun we can't find. Who had the best motive to kill Mr. Hatton?"

Brendan let that question hang there for a few moments while looking at the reactions of everyone in the room.

"When Detective Barone was seeking the location of the recipient of the money Mr. Iverson had given to Hatton, he made another discovery. The amount given to Mrs. Gisriel was significantly more than Iverson's. Hatton had convinced someone else to invest in his real estate scheme. Someone who had been very careful with his money, who had been ridiculed in school, called 'Rufus' and other names and suddenly had the opportunity to throw it back in the face of his neighbor by showing that he had the cash and was going to have Hatton indebted to him. His pride and need for revenge clouded his good sense and he let Hatton court him for many days about the investment before he acquiesced and gave him two thousand dollars. No sooner than he had, he came to his senses and demanded the money back. But it was already gone." Brendan looked at Daugherty, whose face had gone white.

"He knew Hatton's routine because he had walked in the alley before. That day he went out for a walk with his dog with his own rifle tucked beneath his long coat in the cold weather. He confronted Hatton as he came home from work, but his old adversary laughed in his face. Furious, he pulled out the rifle and shot him. There was nothing to give him away but the barking of his dog, which he had to bring home while he called the police. He left the terrified dog at his place and returned to the Hatton house to play the part of the concerned neighbor."

Daugherty's mouth was working although he said nothing at first. "You know what he did! He stole Iverson's money, and he took mine, as well."

"You only gave him your money to show him that your lifelong frugality had paid off and he was not better than you," Brendan said.

"He was always so full of himself. We knew each other as children, and with his teasing and bullying he tormented me. Made fun of my name, called me 'Dogman,' mocked me because of my red hair and my lack of athletic ability. Then the worst was that we were enrolled at the same boarding school, where the agony continued when he enlisted his friends to do the same. I was beaten down, and when it came time to go to college, I made sure I knew where he was going and took myself off to Brown, where things got so much better. He was a terrible person and if anyone had reason to kill him, it was I. But I challenge you to prove that I did." He looked satisfied with himself and at that point Brendan had no additional proof but charged him, nonetheless.

An officer was called in and Daugherty was charged with murder, handcuffed and taken to be officially booked. One by one, the aghast group dispersed, leaving only Dominic, Amanda and Brendan, who closed the door after the last person left.

"My money was on Van Eaton," Barone said. "I don't know if he'll want the widow now that he knows her finances are in shambles."

"Do you think that Mr. Daugherty's years of bullying really could have pushed him to the edge?" Amanda asked.

"It's very possible. But he is also a vulnerable individual and I think with the continual pressure and questioning, he will show his hand and brag about what he did. In the meantime, he won't be able to kill again."

Brendan was correct. Daugherty did indeed brag about what he 'could' have done if he 'had done it.' But the constant interrogation that followed wore him down. More importantly, the thought that his dog would be put down in his absence saddened him and he considered suicide. Once assured that Hector would go to a loving home, he succumbed to the inevitable and confessed.

## Chapter 24

Amanda and Brendan were at Catalano's several days later after life had returned to its almost normal cadence.

Over a bowl of lentil soup with sausage, Amanda asked, "Do you think you'll ever find the gun?"

"Probably not. He was very cagey about where it 'might' be. I did wonder for some time if he had done it because I didn't think he had the courage."

"Who got the other gun out of Saul's pawn shop?"

"Based on Eddie's description, it sounded like a woman trying to pretend to be a man. Who knows? A jealous wife? A wronged girlfriend?"

"In other words, it could have been Mrs. Hatton, Doris, Sally on behalf of her boyfriend, or Florence, the secretary," Amanda said.

"Or some totally unconnected person waiting to take revenge at some point in the future. Or a young woman keen on marksmanship whose parents wouldn't buy her a gun."

"Speaking of weapons, now that I'm pursuing my career as a private investigator…."

"Wait—what? You're not still working for your father?"

"Based on the footwork I did for the Hatton case, the firm has decided to make my position permanent. I just have to get a license, which seems to involve recommendations from reputable people in the community. I'm counting on you to be one of them," she said with a smile.

"That could be a conflict of interest, don't you think?"

"How so?"

"Need I remind you that we are engaged, which indicates that we will be married sooner rather than later. I don't know if an almost-family member's opinion would be taken as unprejudiced. And my interests lie in having you all to myself, not sharing you with a bunch of lowlifes."

"I hope you're not suggesting that I be a stay-at-home wife with nothing to do but cook, clean and have babies," she said.

Brendan paused. "Not just yet."

Amanda looked him in the eyes, trying to see if he was once again teasing her or if he was serious. He gave a bit of a smile, which didn't help her, but she said, "Not just yet by a long shot. We've got a lot of work ahead of us."

## MURDER IN BEACON HILL

Amanda Burnside becomes a bona fide private investigator.
Her first case is helping her sister's boyfriend who has been accused of murder.
Did he do it? Or can she track down the real killer?

## MURDER IN DORCHESTER

Coming September 30, 2024

If you enjoyed this book, please let other readers know. Reviews help readers discover my books, so feel free to leave a short line or two:

## MY REVIEW PAGE

See my website to be notified of more titles:
www.Andreas-books.com

Thank you! Happy Reading,
Andrea

www.ingramcontent.com/pod-product-compliance
Ingram Content Group UK Ltd.
Pitfield, Milton Keynes, MK11 3LW, UK
UKHW020732250925
8076UKWH00024B/277